# JERRY AND RODRIGO GO TO WAR

*Jerry and Rodrigo Go to War: A Novel*
© Steven Salaita

This edition © 2026 Common Notions

This is work is licensed under the Creative Commons Attribution-NonCommercial 4.0 International. To view a copy of this license, visit https://creativecommons.org/licenses/by-nc/4.0/

ISBN: 978-1-945335-46-4 | eBook ISBN: 978-1-945335-72-3
Library of Congress Number: 2026930549

10 9 8 7 6 5 4 3 2 1

Common Notions
PO Box 18823
Philadelphia, PA 19119

commonnotions.org
info@commonnotions.org

Discounted bulk quantities of our books are available for organizing, educational, or fundraising purposes. Please contact Common Notions at the address above for more information.

Cover design by Josh MacPhee
Layout design and typesetting by Suba Murugan
Printed in Canada by Union Labor

# JERRY AND RODRIGO GO TO WAR

A Novel

*Steven Salaita*

*Philadelphia, PA*
*Brooklyn, NY*

## ALSO BY THE AUTHOR

*Anti-Arab Racism in the USA: Where it Comes from and What it Means for Politics* (2006)

*The Holy Land in Transit: Colonialism and the Quest for Canaan* (2006)

*Arab American Literary Fictions Cultures and Politics* (2007)

*The Uncultured Wars* (2008)

*Modern Arab American Fiction: A Reader's Guide* (2011)

*Israel's Dead Soul* (2011)

*Uncivil Rites* (2015)

*Inter/Nationalism: Decolonizing Native America and Palestine* (2016)

*An Honest Living: A Memoir of Peculiar Itineraries* (2024)

*Daughter, Son, Assassin: A Novel* (2024)

# ABOUT THE NONALIGNED SERIES

The Nonaligned Series is dedicated to fiction, literary nonfiction, and poetry that explores the historical and ongoing legacies of anticolonial politics, the evolving nature of imperialism, and the world-making freedom movements of our times. The series highlights vital and creative sources of internationalist imagination within the fractures and fault lines of the current world order. The name takes inspiration from the worldwide anticolonial and anti-imperialist self-determination movements that sparked a wave of decolonization in the 1960s and '70s across Africa, Latin America, Asia, and the Arab world.

For more information about the Nonaligned Series, visit commonnotions.org/nonaligned.

# CONTENTS

# PART I

# 1

Vengeance isn't nearly as easy as movies and books make it seem. I can tell you that firsthand. In fact, I'll go ahead and tell you about it right now.

I once decided to avenge a wrong I had suffered and it changed the way I think about almost everything. Vengeance requires war, but the war is never limited to the main antagonists. See, vengeance isn't really about retribution. That's how it seems on the surface, but in reality it's a kind of cosmic struggle. You seek vengeance and you also go to war against the nature of the entire world.

That's the lesson I took from it, anyway. I reckon it doesn't matter now. Despite the disappointing ending I can say that I'm relieved it's over. Maybe a bit salty, too, but relieved all the same.

Relief doesn't solve anything, though. It's just a feeling that can be good or bad or neutral depending on the situation. It sure as hell doesn't change the fact that I wrote a novel and then Rodrigo stole it from me. I don't know when he did it, and I don't know how he did it, but I guarantee you it damn well happened.

I have to say it from the get-go because what I'm about to tell you won't make any sense otherwise.

Rodrigo Suarez stole my novel. Sear this fact into your brain. Stir it into your porridge with a stick of cinnamon.

Truly a strange, stupid man, that Rodrigo.

Now, I can practically hear you thinking: "Jerry, it's an open-and-shut situation. If he stole your novel, then you have proof. Call his publisher. Hire a lawyer. Worst case, you take to the internet and make his life miserable."

Well, things are a bit more complicated than that.

First of all, he denies it. That's no surprise. You ever hear of a white-collar thief who fesses up? "But what about the proof, Jerry? You have a document, with timestamps." It's true. I do. Get this, though: he says I stole the novel from him. How's that for a punch in the gut?

In fact, bringing claims against Rodrigo caused a lot more problems than it solved. I promised myself I'd never talk about him again, and I had every intention of keeping the promise, but that's the annoying thing about this whole situation: you have to think about a person in order to ignore him.

Believe me when I say he stole my novel, though. Pay attention, because this isn't my story alone. I guarantee you're in here somewhere, too. Villain, architect, instigator, victim–anything, really, but more than just a witness or bystander. Go ahead and settle into something comfortable and let me tell you how it happened.

# 2

I reckon you're good and confused by now. Don't worry, I'm fixing to tell you everything. It's a simple story but it's complicated, too. Stories can be like that. Some of them don't have many characters and a real basic plot, but they still screw with your head. I don't know if this is one of those stories. I'm just saying that maybe it's not as simple as it seems.

I don't know where to start, exactly. Most of the stuff I plan to tell you about happened around six, seven years ago and a lot of events led me to my current position. If I could go back in time, I'd change about half of them and the others I'm happy to have on record, so I can't be too mad in the end: half isn't enough to have changed the outcome.

I suppose it makes most sense to start with Olivia. She didn't have anything to do with Rodrigo, but I became a writer because of her. And there's no story without me having become a writer. Olivia was what I'd call a bit unrefined, for lack of a better word. That doesn't mean poor, exactly. More like she didn't come from money. There's a difference between the two. She wore really loud makeup—purple above the eyes, bright red on the lips—and it gave her the look of a rock star groupie. She reminded me of the girls I grew up with, but I could sense immediately that she wasn't one of them. Don't ask me to explain how I could know it; I just did. I wouldn't have been attracted to her otherwise. I don't have much right to be picky, it's true, but a man likes what he likes and a woman's no different.

Anyway, Olivia was a server at BT's. I was out with my grad school cohort. It was nothing fancy, just Radford. It's a regional university in Southwest Virginia if you don't know it, down the road from Virginia Tech, in a town even smaller than Blacksburg. We were all first-year MAs in the English program back in the late nineties. I'd done my undergrad there and stayed on for a master's after I found out that you get a tuition waiver and monthly stipend for teaching a few courses. Teaching seemed like an easy gig. Fresh out of undergrad, I figured I knew better than anyone how to run a class.

At first the cohort was like a family. The camaraderie didn't last long—most of us hated each other by the middle of the second semester, which was the only realistic aspect of the whole family thing. There were about six of us at BT's that night. It was a small cohort, ten total, if memory serves, and two of them were geriatrics who had no desire to hang out. It was the early days of the internet and cell phones and there was no social media so we spent a lot of time at the bar. On that night I had four vodkas under my belt—heavy grog probably distilled in an industrial park—and was about to switch to equally dubious tequila when Olivia shimmied up to our table.

"Hey, everybody, I'm taking over your table for the night. What can I . . . ? Oh my God! Ms. Steele?"

"I told y'all to call me Missy!"

Missy was from Tazewell, deep in Southwest Virginia. She seemed delighted to be recognized. That was the coolest thing about teaching, I guess. It gave us the chance to be local celebrities.

Olivia looked embarrassed. I didn't understand what was so weird about running into a teacher at the bar. Do people think that teachers don't exist outside the classroom? That they don't shop and eat out like everyone else? Maybe it's because Olivia had to serve her teacher. Even then, so what? She served all kinds of people who were important in their own tiny universes. She knew this one, that's all.

I found Olivia's embarrassment damn-near irresistible. She was obviously a freshman, or else Missy wouldn't have been her teacher. Even though she didn't fit the typical definition of hot according to the college male calculus, I was instantly turned on. It was the way she carried herself, coy and suggestive and dramatic. At first glance she seemed like a standard college girl, the kind you would find on any campus from Miami to Seattle. But I looked closer: her smile was filled with mischief and her eyes, looking almost gray beneath the bright mascara, were all kinds of frisky. She didn't look a single bit boring, I can promise you that.

After she scampered off, Missy pretended to be mortified.

"It's, like, so weird, ain't it?"

Everyone nodded and agreed. Except me. I was thinking about how to chat up the server without Missy finding out. Like everyone in the cohort, Missy was dying for a chance to rescue one of her students. All the better if she had to fend off a horny man. We were way into our students' business. Our jobs didn't begin and end in the classroom. More than anything we wanted to teach those little fuckers about life. Their personal drama was like a precious resource. Our own professors who taught us about teaching gave off this vibe like we were more life coach than composition instructor. One of them even gave a speech about the grammar of good citizenship.

Let me tell you something about good citizenship: it's a load of horseshit. Show me a good citizen and I'll show you a first-class sucker. The way I see it, we'd become a society of robots if it weren't for the delinquents considerate enough to break some laws.

We would sit at BT's for hours, bitching about ungrateful students and moaning about a million problems that were pretty much unsolvable. There were never answers because we weren't raising any real questions. We were learning how to become martyrs.

Well, I'll tell you, I was never into it. I wanted to hold my classes and then get on with life.

Problem was, getting on with life meant hanging out with my cohort, a mixture of dorks, duds, and dumbasses. Radford was familiar territory, but its grad school subculture was new to me. I'd done undergrad at Radford, but as soon as I became an MA student, things changed with my old friends. By that point most had flunked out and those who were still around stuck to their own kind. Grad school was its own little world. My old friends wanted no part of it and, to be frank, I didn't want them anywhere near it, either.

I didn't love that little world, but can't say I hated it, either. I was just trying to make something of myself. Nobody thought I had it in me back home, but that wasn't a problem anymore. The cohort didn't know if I was smart and would have felt guiltier than all hell for thinking me stupid. To them I was just another guy with big dreams of intellectual glory. I knew at the time that they were way too earnest and well-meaning for academic success. They were always on about human rights and voting rights and abortion rights and every other right except the kind that exists opposite of wrong. The evil of binary oppositions was a big thing back then.

The grammar of good citizenship. Fuck that.

Sorry for the tangent. I do that sometimes.

Where was I?

That's right. Olivia. I wanted to see her again. She'd done a number on me. So I started going to BT's for lunch. It was the only time I could be sure my friends wouldn't be around. Sooner or later the girl would have to work a day shift, I reasoned. It looked like I'd be wrong about that one. I went to BT's ten days in a row and she was nowhere to be found. My stipend wasn't big enough for eating out more than twice a week, so after a few days I stuck to the bar. Day-drinking wasn't a problem for me and I wasn't putting much down, anyway. Owing to my thin finances, I stretched out each beer until my patience dried up.

I was about to call it quits one day when I saw her working the upstairs section.

"You know what? I'm feelin' kinda hungry," I told the bartender, who was starting to feel like a friend.

"I'll get you a menu," he said.

"Shit, I don't wanna hang around here and eat on this filthy bar. I'm gettin' a table."

I ran off before he could get offended and seated myself in the corner, as far from the other diners as I could get. The room wasn't inviting. The dim lighting didn't seem like it was on purpose, for ambiance or whatever. The place used cheap bulbs, something most college students wouldn't notice. Dark wooden tables only added to the gloom. Olivia came over and dropped a paper coaster on the table.

"Hello," she said, full of smiles, but I knew that she was dying to get out of there and have some fun. I could see it in the gray of her eyes. "Will anyone be joining you today?"

"Nah, I'm makin' notes for class," I said, tapping the Norton anthology I'd set out on the table. "A class I'm teachin'," I clarified.

Her expression didn't change, so I moved on to plan B. Squinting my eyes and cocking my head, I looked up at her.

"You look familiar."

She shrugged and began tapping her foot.

"I know," I said, slapping my forehead. "You're in my colleague Missy's class."

Her foot stopped tapping. She said hopefully, "Ms. Steele?"

"That's right. She's a good friend of mine."

She looked long and hard at the seat across from me. "I love Ms. Steele."

"Yeah, she's great. Say, what's your name, anyway?"

"Olivia."

"I knew it! I knew you seemed familiar. I could just guess it was you. Missy talks about you all the time."

Her chin just about crashed onto the table. She assumed that Missy's talk was good. I liked that about her.

"She does?"

"She sure does."

I was about to go on, but both of us could feel one of her other tables getting impatient. A few passive-aggressive eggheads were clearing their throats and tapping their glasses against the tabletop.

"Sorry, I gotta go take care of another table. What can I get you to drink?"

"Seltzer water would be fine."

I'd planned out the answer. Soda didn't feel very professorial and ordering booze at lunchtime might make her think I was a drunkard. Seltzer water seemed safe and reasonable, like a liquid version of Canada or something.

A few minutes later she returned with the drink and asked what I want to eat. I could tell she wanted to keep talking about Missy but was afraid of sounding too eager or needy. That was exactly how I wanted her to feel, so I ordered a club sandwich and went back to my anthology. Olivia hesitated and then went away to put in the order.

She lingered after bringing the food. The group of professors had paid out. She only had one more table, a couple that clearly didn't want to be bothered.

"I wish you could sit and join me," I said, gesturing to the chair across from me.

"Me, too. But I'm not allowed."

"That's a real shame. One reason I got into teachin' is so I wouldn't have a boss houndin' me all the time with stupid rules."

"Tell me about it."

"Seems like you might have what it takes, accordin' to Missy."

Hearing the name made her blush again. "No way."

"It's true. You have a few things to clean up, but she's really impressed with you overall."

"I need to clean stuff up?"

Who knew she'd get hung up on the negative?

"Well, you know," I said, "there's always areas for improvement."

"Like what?"

"I'm not exactly sure, but I'll take a guess. Like with my students, one problem I always see is that they like to make an argument as if there's no opposin' view. They just ramble on and on like their opinion's the only one in the world. Okay, well, how would you answer to this other point of view? What do other people think about this stuff? Get what I'm sayin'? Missy prolly sees the same problem. She's always complainin' that her students don't know how to consider different viewpoints."

"I can see other points of view."

"I'm sure you can."

"I think I do, anyway. Hold on, maybe I don't."

"It ain't always so clear."

"I'll try harder to do it on my next response paper."

"Missy'd be mightily impressed."

"How do I know if I'm doing it right?"

"I reckon you'd need somebody with professional trainin' to give you some feedback."

She twisted her lips and narrowed her eyes. I knew what she was thinking. I also knew that she wouldn't be up-front about it.

"I guess I could try the writing center," she said.

"The writin' center?" I laughed. "Hell, they're useless. They don't help with anything. Their whole philosophy is encouragin' students to do it all themselves. They won't even edit a typo."

"What do I do, then?"

Luckily for her, I had a couple of ideas.

A few days later she was sitting next to me, a paper draft on my desk. It wasn't the best situation because I didn't have a real office: all of us graduate teaching fellows shared a large room divided into cubicles, with a clanky little fridge near the door. The room was halfway underground and smelled like day-old air conditioning. You could practically see the mold spores floating through the air. I'd have preferred someplace more private, but didn't want to scare off Olivia.

We looked over her draft, our foreheads almost touching, and our mouths close enough to exchange the same air. I had a hell of a time holding back my feelings, but Olivia seemed normal. Her brows were furrowed and she chewed at the corner of her bottom lip. After we finished–she had picked up most of what I showed her, but she wasn't exactly a prodigy–I was tempted to pat her on the shoulder, but thought better of it. She grinned and thanked me and I made her promise to report back.

As Olivia walked away, I could see Missy glaring at me from above a partition across the way. A few seconds later I heard her footsteps moving across the room. She popped her head into my cubicle and looked none too happy.

"Gerald Turley, what in the world are you doin' with my student?"

She acted like we were kin even though we didn't know each other before grad school. We probably ran into one another a few times in undergrad–Missy went to Hollins, up the road in Roanoke–but if it happened neither of us remembered. She felt an affinity for me because I grew up one town over from Tazewell, in a place called Bluefield, which is just like Tazewell except the border to West Virginia runs through it. Radford had a lot of people from Southwest Virginia, but the English graduate program was mostly a northern affair. Missy expected me to understand her in a certain way. I was okay doing it so long as she didn't reciprocate.

"Oh, hey, Missy," I said, trying to look startled. "I didn't know you was here."

She gave me this look like she was trying to figure out my angle, but I wasn't worried that she'd succeed, even with an angle as obvious as mine. She kept her arms crossed but her expression softened.

"Why wouldn't she come to me for help?" Missy said, then slid onto the seat Olivia had been in.

I patted her shoulder. "Hell, Missy, you know how intimidatin' it can be visitin' a professor's office hours."

"Not really."

"C'mon now. Not all students are as self-confident as you were."

"Hm, I never thought of it that way."

"Yeah, some of these kids can be pretty shy. They ain't like our generation."

"I guess you're right."

"Besides, writin' can be real scary to a lot of people. Not everyone's as comfortable with it as you are."

I figured the more I got Missy talking about herself the less I'd have to worry that she would talk about Olivia. Because, believe me, I tried and tried and couldn't think of a single good reason why the girl would have come to me for tutoring. Sure enough, Missy got stuck on her special talents as a student. It wasn't too hard to nudge her in that direction because all of us kids from Southwest Virginia were secretly insecure about our intellectual ability even at a hole like Radford. The place was filled with preppies and hipsters who attended fancy high schools in Northern Virginia. They'd catch our accent and suddenly act like we were imbeciles. It probably didn't help Missy's confidence that Olivia was obviously from Nova.

Anyway.

You're probably waiting for the part where I'm in bed with Olivia, but that's the damndest thing about this story: it never happened. She made an A on the paper and it killed my chances. Suddenly she was smitten with writing and filled with a sense of purpose. She ended up being exactly like the version of herself that I invented. She became Missy's star student and then signed up as an English major. By junior year she was working in the writing center. No tips, but no grab-ass sleazebags like the ones who frequent BT's, either. A clear upgrade.

She wasn't the only one who learned a thing or two about writing, though. Despite not getting anywhere with Olivia, I accomplished something that was even more exciting: I created an honest-to-God character. I gave her a personality and a mission. I even made her look a certain way. And then she became real. Olivia wasn't my muse; she was my prototype.

# 3

Now, you might think that getting a graduate degree in English helped me be more creative. If so, you'd be wrong. Majoring in English has about as much to do with creativity as shoveling the driveway has to do with skiing.

I chose English because I enjoy reading. It seemed like a good deal that I could get a degree doing the same thing I'd be doing if I didn't go to college. Reading seems like a funny habit for someone like me, a bona fide yokel. But I always enjoyed it just the same even though I never really thought about becoming a writer until I met Olivia. People in Bluefield didn't consider writing a real job. To them, a writer was either broke or above his raisin'. Or some kind of queer or commie. There wasn't any way to be a respectable middle-class writer unless you covered sports.

After the Olivia thing, I said to myself, "Goddammit, Jerry, you're good at telling stories. Ever since you was little you could lie with the best of 'em." And so I aimed to do something with that skill. I wasn't at a fancy MFA program and was saddled with my mountain drawl, but I was determined to give it a try, anyway. Just like I can tell different stories, I can use different languages in the telling. They call it code-switching. I call it being more versatile than the assholes up north.

I didn't have any other choice, really. In Bluefield, storytelling wasn't a pastime; it was a survival skill. A lot of people can spin a good yarn, but not all of them can make it believable. You can't always gab your way into believability. You have to tell a story with your expression, with your eye movements, with your posture. Sometimes you have to tell it with a document.

I was fifteen the first time I told a good story. I wasn't thinking about anything literary; I was just trying to avoid trouble. And that connection stayed with me because writing to survive is the only way it'll be worth a shit. You can always tell the difference between a milksop and a scrapper, somebody desperate to put food on the table or to express something eating him up real good inside.

Well, the only thing eating me up in those days was Rodrigo, but it was enough to give me all the edge I needed. I had to bleed and sweat for my stories and he took them from me. He didn't just steal my novel; he stole my whole damn history.

But we'll get to Rodrigo later.

I was fixing to tell you about my first good story before he showed up in my brain again.

# 

It comes down to this: I had it pretty rough when I was a kid. My daddy was a railroad worker who was hardly home before he ran off for good when I was in second grade. My mama didn't waste any time finding his replacement. By the time I was in third grade I had a stepdaddy by the name of Ronnie. As you probably guessed, Ronnie was a no-good son of a bitch. My real daddy wasn't much better, but somehow the abuse isn't as bad when it's your own blood dishing it out.

Ronnie dipped spearmint Skoal and drank Milwaukee's Best. He used to send me over to the Short Stop to get him new provisions every few days. I always made sure to palm a little something for myself. We lived in West Graham, a pretty rundown area. Our house had rotted wood siding and a leaky roof and even though Ronnie was supposed to be handy I don't ever remember him trying to fix anything. When he was at home, he sat in a filthy recliner with his shirt off and watched ESPN, taking a break every now and again to bark orders. He wasn't home much, though. He spent a lot of time fishing and hunting and drinking with his buddies at Cotton's.

Ronnie was always hot and flustered. I used to hate seeing him with his shirt off because a million wet dark hairs would be matted across his belly. It didn't make any sense to me. His beard was patchy and light brown, like the long hair on his head. But on his chest and stomach the hair was almost black. I had to pretend that Ronnie was a father of some kind, but nobody could stop me from being happy that I didn't inherit his genes.

He had this way of holding a belt so that the buckle landed rather than the strap and he didn't limit his aim to the backside. He hit arms and legs and sometimes he got some face, too, both mine and mama's. I screamed a lot; she took her beatings without a word. She worked in the packaging department at Quik Café and didn't seem to have much energy after work. If Ronnie wanted to whoop me, then it was his prerogative and my problem. I'm not too mad at her. She found the same kind of household she was raised in. To her a regular beating was normal.

I disagreed. It was normal, all right, but I didn't think it should have been. The older I got, the more I began to hate Ronnie. I couldn't think of any good he did for the world. He was a bum who sucked up oxygen from more deserving animals.

When I was fifteen, I tagged along on one of his hunting trips. He had a friend who owned some land in Giles County. I was decked out in the proper gear, but Ronnie said that blaze orange is for pussies. He wore camouflage head to toe. I knew he'd shush me if I reminded him that deer are colorblind, so I kept my mouth shut. It wasn't a problem for me if he wanted to look like GI Joe.

We barely talked as we creeped through the woods, the ground soggy with rotting leaves. I was in no hurry. I followed Ronnie as he looked for game, pretending to be some kind of nature boy who could read broken twigs and sniff animal piss. After we went a couple of hours without so much as seeing a rodent, I started to get impatient.

After I felt certain that nobody was around, I aimed my shotgun at Ronnie and waited for him to notice. He walked ahead of me about ten yards and then turned around.

He spit out a rope of snuff juice and snarled, "What the hell you think you're doin', boy?"

I walked toward him with the gun still in position.

"Put down the gun you crazy little fa–"

I filled his face with buckshot before he could finish the sentence.

I kicked up an enormous racket even before making sure he was dead. I screamed for help as I tore through the woods. By the time paramedics reached the scene, Ronnie was ready to be hauled away without any hurry.

It was the kind of accident that happened regularly in those days. Ronnie was scouting a buck and I was set to take it down if it crossed in my direction. But I was inexperienced and jumpy. I didn't know anything about hunting, not like the grizzled men who trawl those hills, anyway.

"Your old man put you in a bad position," the guys at the police station told me.

Poor Ronnie. He should have worn blaze orange.

I used to think that storytelling is supposed to be enjoyable, so I never figured that my ability to bullshit might make me some kind of artist. In time I learned that violence is no stranger to pleasure. All of us writers are the same type of scumbag. Some of us just have the right pedigree to fool the liberal nitwits in the big city.

Knowing you can write and becoming a writer are very different things. Hell, they're usually at loggerheads. I doubt that all those pencil dicks who pump out bestsellers are such terrible writers by accident. They know how to write terribly for profit. If your main priority is making a good book, then it's not easy to become a published author.

Or you could steal someone else's work. It's not something I ever could bring myself to do. I sure didn't like it when I was the victim. The worst thing about it is that having a story stolen gave me a lot more stories, but none of them is a damn bit believable.

# 5

The gulf between wanting to write a good book and actually writing a good book makes the Grand Canyon look like a sidewalk crack. It took me around two decades to write my first (and only) novel. It's not that I wasn't trying. I was stuck in the world's most uninspiring setting.

After I finished my MA, I did a lot of bumming around. I planned to hang out in Radford until I ran out of money, which I figured to happen before the end of summer, and then busy myself finding ways to make it. There was plenty to do in the meantime. None of it was productive, but that didn't bother me. The way I see it, there are dozens of ways to be productive that don't involve spit-shining somebody's shoes or scrubbing shit off a toilet seat. Why, smoking dope and getting laid are some of the most productive things a person can do. Pleasure ain't supposed to go with violence and it ain't supposed to go with work. That tells you how messed up the world is. Unless you're rich, being miserable is the only kind of good citizenship.

Well, that's what I was doing the summer after graduation, weed and women. Radford had both in abundance. The weed was often schwag and the women weren't exactly Jackie O, but bad weed is still good energy and none of the women complained about my productivity. Right around the beginning of August, I got a call from the supervisor of the GTF program. Radford had increased enrollment and there weren't enough people to teach freshman comp. Would I be interested in picking up a few classes?

I wanted to know why he called me and he said that I had distinguished myself among the cohort, which I took to mean that nobody else in my cohort was available. I had spent the last two years teaching composition, so it seemed like an easy gig. I'd just have to revise the dates on my syllabi. I said sure and not long after found myself at new employee orientation, which, based on my level of misery, was an extremely productive two days. And just like that, I was a member of the faculty.

Maybe calling myself a member of the faculty is stretching things. Technically I was part of the faculty and the chair and dean made it a point to call me a colleague—too much of a point, as far as I was concerned. If they really saw me as a colleague, then they would have been a lot ruder. In reality, I was at the lowest point of the institutional hierarchy—not even an adjunct, just a contract instructor. I couldn't vote on anything and would be out of a job if enrollment went down. The pay was terrible but I'd learned to survive in Radford on a limited budget.

On the first day of class, I walked in five minutes late and spent another five shuffling through papers while the students glanced awkwardly at one another. I finally stood and adjusted the lectern.

"Mornin'. My name is Professor Turley. You can call me Professor Turley." Those little shits didn't know the difference between a contract teacher and an endowed chair. "Over the course of this semester," I continued, "y'all are gonna learn to write at a college level."

A hand went up.

"Yes?" I said, pointing to a girl in pajama bottoms and a tight pink undershirt.

"Aren't you, like, young to be a professor?"

"How young do you think I am?"

"I don't know."

"Well, I must be really damn smart to have become a professor at my age."

Some of the students giggled. They always do when a professor cusses for the first time. The girl wanted to say something else, but I got on with class. I dropped a stack of stapled syllabi on the desk closest to me and said, "Grab one, pass 'em on."

I read aloud and stopped after each section to ask if there were any questions. There weren't. I'd learn that there never are. Instructors obsess over syllabi but students don't care about them and you can't change their minds no matter how much you plead. They want to know one of two things: what exactly will it take for me to make an A, minimum threshold? And, when are the papers due (according to late policy)? Sure, there are exceptions. Even a podunk campus like Radford will have overachievers, but on balance students are students, the same no matter which crest adorns their hoodies.

As a GTF, I had to run everything past a faculty mentor, but now I was on my own. I didn't like having a mentor. Mine was into group work, which is the dumbest thing I ever heard of. Most everything struck me as dumb, in fact. You have to think like a student, not a teacher. Group work sounds okay in theory. In reality, it leads to one person doing everything while the others pretend to be shy. If you do a group assignment, it's even worse. I wasn't about to listen to a bunch of kids whine about their useless classmates. My students would pass or fail on their own merits.

That's what I told myself, anyway. In reality, I went soft on the grading and got softer as the years passed. I won't sit here and argue that laziness had nothing to do with it, but there was no incentive to be a tough grader, not that I wanted to be some kind of hardass or whatever. Contract teachers are hired based on enrollment, but they're retained based on student evaluations, which are based on a lot of things that have fuck-all to do with quality of teaching. Is the teacher ugly? Lower evaluations. Does the teacher wear jeans? Higher evaluations. Does the teacher cuss? Higher evaluations. Is there a lot of work? Lower evaluations. High grades equal high evaluations. High evaluations equal not getting fired. You don't have to be John Nash to figure it out.

I never had a problem thinking of teaching as a form of customer service. Lots of professors get pissy about the comparison, but you can't really complain when colleges make hiring decisions based on the equivalent of a Yelp review. The way I see it, if you want to change the model of higher education then you'd better get to working on a new society altogether. And since professors will never sign off on any kind of society but the current one, they ought to just let it go. They're not wired to relax, that's the problem. And too many rubes out in the world think that having a PhD makes a person worth listening to.

Sorry, another tangent.

Back to my first class.

After I finished the syllabus, which took about fifteen minutes, the students got antsy. They figured there was nothing else to do on the first day. They started packing up their stuff and inching their asses off the plastic seats.

"Hold on," I said. "We're gonna do a little icebreaker." They grumbled and reset their haunches.

"What's an icebreaker?" the girl in pajama bottoms asked.

"It's a getchaknowya."

She looked at me stupidly.

"The icebreaker is called fact or fiction," I went on. "Here's how it works: you tell us a bit about yourself—name, hometown, stuff like that—and then offer up a fact about your life. It can be true or it can be false. Everyone else gets to decide."

Some of the students nodded in approval. Others looked suspicious.

"I'll go first: my name is Professor Turley, this is my third year teachin' at Radford, and I've been to war eight different times."

They smirked and wrote their answers.

"You. Go," I said, pointing to a girl in the front left of the classroom.

"Um, okay. Like, my name is Angie and, um, I'm from, like, Newport News and so, yeah, um, my fact or fiction is that I'm from Newport News."

"Well done," I said. "Next."

It went on like that for a while. The kids were either indifferent or terrible liars and I couldn't rightly believe that they made it to college without knowing how to lie at least a little bit.

"Yeah, my name is Dave," began a kid in a Rehoboth Beach T-shirt. "I'm from Reston, no major yet. My fact or fiction is that I moonlight as a porn actor."

"Liar," a girl called out.

"Here, I can prove it to you," Dave said, sliding over in his seat as if to stand.

"That won't be necessary," I said, wagging my finger.

It was then I decided to add icebreakers to the list of useless shit.

After everyone had revealed whether their fact was true or not, I dismissed class with the intention of running out ahead of the students. They didn't move, though.

"What about yours, professor? Fact or fiction?"

"Oh, sorry, I forgot. Mine happens to be fact."

"What? No way."

"A fact's a fact," I said before strolling out of the room.

I wasn't lying, either. War is a little town up in McDowell County, about an hour from Bluefield.

I always remember that session not only because it was the first class I taught, but also because it was the beginning of a temporary situation that never ended. My plan was to teach to pay the bills until I became a writer, just until I made it big. Then I wouldn't have to worry about babysitting undergrads and delivering good service. I'd be my own man, answering to nobody but the fickle gods of craft and generations of unborn readers.

It didn't happen that way. Not even close.

# 6

Thinking of my first class as a teacher brings back to mind my first class as a student. The two couldn't have been more different. Both happened at Radford, but the similarities end there.

It was an 8 a.m. intro to world religions. An elective, I believe, but it fulfilled a core requirement. I must have picked it over sociology or psychology or something, but I couldn't tell you why. Religion probably sounded more real or legitimate.

The class was in an old repurposed chapel near the dorms. My memory is a bit fuzzy, but I recall a humid and crowded room and lots of yawning. I also recall being nervous. See, I didn't know anything about religion. I don't mean like beliefs and rituals and whatnot; I mean religion as a fact that exists in the world and is an important part of people's daily lives. In retrospect, I could have used those sociology and psychology courses.

I knew hardly anything about my own religion except that it was mainstream in Bluefield. We were just regular Christians who used grape juice for communion and stayed seated throughout the service. Not that my family went to church. In our household, Sunday mornings were for hangovers and eating Apple Jacks in our underwear. I never considered the possibility that being Christian was anything but normal. When you take a second to think about it, which nobody did because thinking can lead to a whole lot of trouble, we normal Christians accepted some real nutty stuff as true and it could only be seen as true because all the nutty stuff other people believed was so obviously false.

I figured I'd be in trouble if the professor expected us to know anything about the material off the bat. We didn't have much world religion where I grew up. There were some immigrant families, mostly doctors, but the old-time townsfolk never bothered to learn where or how they worshipped. We knew that the immigrants weren't all the same–they had different skin colors, different hair, different clothes, different languages–but in the end they all fit into the same big category of foreign. Our aim back in those days was to make life simple. We didn't understand–and still don't understand–that simplicity for one group of people makes things complicated for everyone else. Or maybe we understood and just didn't give a damn.

All of this is to say I wasn't rightly prepared for the religion class. I balanced it out by being unprepared for college in general.

Usually in this kind of story, the professor comes in and blows everyone's mind. There's a lot of introspection, some soul-searching, bright pinwheels spinning inside of eyeballs and then, boom, a life-changing epiphany. Kids walk into the room as run-of-the-mill dipshits and walk out transformed into deep thinkers. Not in my story, though. The professor showed up in various shades of beige which clashed with his ruddy skin and immediately began the lesson. No icebreaker, no chitchat, nothing. Just a monotone recital of the syllabus and a few anecdotes about his belief in God. It wasn't a passionate belief, either. More like it was something he did because he was taught to do it and just accepted God as judge of the universe. There was no substance or excitement to it, I guess you could say. He was a serious man who would impart to us the textbook aspects of the world's major religions.

Even with my nervousness and ignorance, I wanted to ask him about all the other stuff, you know, spirituality and cults and polytheism, the stuff we never hear about. "Like, what about Indian religions, American Indian, I mean," I almost said out loud before thinking better of it. Nobody wants to be the guy who keeps asking questions that extend class even if the professor never ends class early on his own. Something in my brain had been activated. It wasn't knowledge. It couldn't have been knowledge. I knew nothing about anything. Hell, it couldn't even be called curiosity because I didn't know what I wanted to learn. I can't really explain it–I guess it was something inside of me that I never knew existed. An instinct, maybe, a weird sensation like I'd been through the course already and found it uninspiring. So I kept my mouth shut.

I went hard on myself for being a chickenshit, but looking back on the situation I think that my silence came from something other than fear. I had worked out that the tribal stuff wasn't real to the professor. He didn't notice it, or know about it to the degree that he knew that he didn't notice it. Maybe he knew about it but didn't consider it serious enough to be a proper religion, just some cute superstition, some exotic way of life that the civilized world had outgrown. He probably didn't know much beyond book learning in general. The interesting stuff, like the religions that never grew beyond a few villages and don't have any hymnals, that don't create pain and conflict and then preach about avoiding exactly what they put into the world, that don't create utopias in other dimensions because they can't find anything worth redeeming on the actual Earth.

I guess I'm saying that from the get-go, the classroom didn't feel like any kind of sanctum. Nope. It felt more like a tomb.

As it happens, I'd experienced that sensation before. The first time, I was a little guy still. I must have been because it wasn't long after Ronnie moved in. He was beside himself when he found out that I didn't know how to swim, so at the beginning of summer he offered to teach me. I was happy as could be. Everyone else knew how to swim, it seemed, and I figured to miss out on lots of fun unless I caught up. It was the last time I remember thinking that things might work out with this Ronnie character.

He drove me to Harmony Acres on a cool and overcast day. I was giddy on the way over. "Settle your ass down," Ronnie had to tell me. I sat on my hands to keep from tapping on the dashboard. As soon as Ronnie stopped the truck I hopped down and ran toward the entrance.

The pool at Harmony Acres was a big circle with a smaller circular platform in the middle holding a low and high dive. It attracted a pretty rough element. Anybody could pay a few dollars and get in for the day, so it was usually crowded. Owing to the bad weather, it was mostly empty that morning. I walked to the edge of the shallow end but Ronnie steered me to the other side. I waited for him to hop in so he could catch me when I jumped, but instead I got a whack between my shoulder blades and the next thing I knew I was underwater. I flailed around trying to reach the surface. The cold water made my lungs feel like peanuts. A few times I made some progress toward the surface, but on the whole I was moving closer to the bottom.

Nobody came to rescue me. I guess the lifeguards were flirting at the snack bar with the local debutantes and everyone else was minding their own business. The water was clear but I only saw darkness, as if trapped in a barrel.

But my little mind started to process big questions. I felt it suddenly and profoundly, the kinetic water somehow a perfect backdrop to my steely desperation, this sense of wanting to be somebody. I was a nobody in a nothing town on the edge of nowhere. I dreamed of breathing again, of growing into an adult, of doing something meaningful before I died. I could see some of the world above the water, colorless, unsteady, and thrashed like mad toward the distortion. Goddammit, I wanted to live. I wanted a purpose and an identity. I wanted my life to matter.

Somebody came and saved me. Or I managed to save myself. I still don't know how it happened. At some point before dying I ended up on the concrete, coughing up all the acid in my stomach.

# 7

Two decades on, I was still teaching freshman comp at Radford. My economic circumstances had changed a bit. After three years of temporary work, I got a long-term contract as an instructor. I couldn't really move up the chain without a PhD, but I was considered a proper member of the department. The pay was still shit, but the true value of the job was security. Colleges are big on symbolic wealth. I was stuck with a 4/4 load and no possibility of sabbatical. Usually I was assigned three comp sections and one 200-level survey, in which I was expected to cover a few centuries of literature inside of fifteen weeks. I hate surveys. They're hard to teach and seem disrespectful to the writers we're supposed to celebrate. Students prefer them over deep dives into Melville, though.

I'd like to blame busyness for my failure to become a published novelist, but I've already told you that I'm good at time management. Pretty much all professors use busyness as an excuse for indolence or indifference. I was plenty busy, even with all the free A's I handed out, but it's not why I didn't become a published novelist. I didn't have anything to publish. My mind was shot. I couldn't come up with any good ideas. On those rare occasions when I did, they wouldn't go very far. I'd start writing and then get bored. I hate to admit it, but the boredom was a manifestation of insecurity. I didn't think I was doing anything worth getting done.

Like so many other instructors with big dreams, I got lost in the rhythm of campus life. The academic calendar dictated all my habits and movements. The calendar is supposed to be a source of freedom, with its big winter and summer breaks, but somehow it manages to be stingy. There's always something going on that has nothing to do with contractual obligations. Socializing, mostly, which isn't how normal people socialize. When I worked at Taco Loco in high school, we socialized by smoking weed out by the grease dumpster and getting sloppy drunk after shutting down. In academe, socializing consisted of passive-aggressive repartee on lawn chairs and floral couches. It's constant, too. You're forever pulled into voluntary activities that in reality are thought of as more important than a colon probe. Socializing is part of the culture. If you don't entertain, or refuse to be entertained, then you're cooked. That's just how people are. You're allowed to be reclusive if you're famous; it's part of the charm. Everyone else has to chitchat and glad-hand. Teaching college is more of a lifestyle than a job. What academics think of as work is meeting friends for drinks or getting together for dinner, stuff that everyone else considers recreation. I knew that if I didn't publish a novel, then becoming reclusive was out of the question.

Anyway, there was little to inspire me in Radford as far as writing went. Sex and booze, never in short supply, aren't inspiration for making art; they're the rewards of being an artist. So the years passed and after a while I had saved enough to move from my rental on the "dark side" of campus, what we used to call the "Deli Mart side," to a small house in the townie area, out beyond the "light side," near the old hospital. It wasn't too different than a typical house back in West Graham, in Bluefield, although I kept it in better condition. I didn't like that I had barely moved beyond my childhood. And I didn't like anything that reminded me of Ronnie.

It wasn't unusual for people to get an MA at Radford and then stay on as an instructor. A bunch of my colleagues were Radford grads. Missy and I were the only ones from our cohort who did it, though. One classmate went on to a doctoral program in Tennessee. The rest wandered into all kinds of things that have nothing to do with English. Missy thought it was cool that two kids from Tazewell County were teaching in the same department. I played along, but never could get excited by regional pride.

Missy didn't get that not everyone from Southwest Virginia is the same. There are Black people and white people, poor people and rich people, semi-normal people and batshit hillbilly people. I didn't see much to be proud about. Back in Bluefield, we had a boy who used to drive his motorcycle to middle school. On the one hand, that's pretty cool; on the other hand, it's still a story about a sixteen-year-old eighth-grader.

Along with English, Missy taught courses in Appalachian Studies. She tried to get me into it. You're from the real Appalachia, she would say, not like all these people from Pennsylvania and Ohio who pretend they're mountain folk. You'd be a natural.

One day I asked her what constitutes mountain folk. I got a bunch of jibber-jabber in return.

"That don't sound like me," I said. "I've never picked at a banjo. I've never been on no goddamn mule."

"Ugh, you've completely missed the point, Jerrah."

"I ain't Appalachian because I do things. It's just where I was born."

"That's the whole point. Your experiences as an Appalachian are authentic. They don't have to be a certain way."

"Let me ask you: what if I talked like Austin Powers and drove a BMW?"

"But you're not like that."

I shook my head. "Let me tell you somethin', Missy, just bein' honest: I think the whole field is fake."

She scrunched her lips into a scowl and didn't talk to me for another two, three weeks. It's funny that my approval was so important to her because in time I became something she needed to outgrow. The field's legitimacy depended on my buy-in and that made me more authentic than any birth certificate or cultural practice. Missy didn't like the tension; she thought it meant conflict rather than growth. There was a moment in time when we could have become a couple, or at least friends with benefits. She was okay-looking, downright pretty after a few drinks, but there was something aggressively unsexual about our relationship. I always suspected that getting with Missy would feel like fucking a first cousin. There's only so much authenticity I'm willing to tolerate.

While I was closing down bars, Missy started a PhD at Virginia Tech in Rhetoric and Composition. She was the darling of English and Appalachian Studies on our campus. With the right degree, both programs would put her on the tenure track. I didn't enjoy that kind of support, especially because you can't hide your activities in a town as tiny as Radford. I regularly crossed paths with students, and plenty of colleagues saw me working the early stages of a one-night stand.

Around the time I was supposed to have been settling down and starting a family, Missy got her hood and, as expected, landed a real job at Radford. They designed an ad with her in mind and went through the entire dog-and-pony show of a national search. Even the dean was in on it. I wasn't upset. Setting up as a loyal and beloved community member at a third-rate university seemed like Missy's destiny from the moment I met her. She would chide me for a lack of ambition, but she didn't know about my aspirations as a novelist. I never told anyone. It didn't seem right to claim the title of writer when I hadn't written anything.

Missy's nagging got me to thinking about the whole Appalachian thing. Was there something about my hometown that made it distinct from similar-sized towns in other rural areas? I couldn't come up with anything that happened in Bluefield that couldn't have happened anywhere else, although the atmosphere framing those events, wild winding mountains and the detritus of a dead coal economy, was close to unique. Maybe that's what made the place exceptional: those long ridges always in the background, blocking half the sky, black in winter and fiercely lush in other seasons.

East River Mountain ran alongside Bluefield on both the West Virginia and Virginia side. When I was a kid, I didn't pay attention to when it ended. I assumed it kept on going until it didn't, wherever that was. It wasn't until high school that I noticed where it tapers off, right around Springville, a supposed town about five miles away from Bluefield on the way to Tazewell. I say "supposed" because it has an elementary school and not much else, just a few meandering roads lined with little houses.

I had a million things on my mind, so I can't say why I noticed the geography on that particular day. The main thing on my mind was the fight I was about to get into. It was the last day of eleventh grade and I was going to Carter Grocery, a convenience store off of 460 in Springville. A classmate named Heath would be meeting me there.

We were fixing to rumble. It had been the talk of the school for two weeks.

Heath had shown up in town halfway through the year. We never did get to know much about him, only that he was a huge prick. He wore a black leather jacket with diagonal zippers on the chest and a matching baseball cap. (We pointed out that he looked like one of the customers at the Blue Oyster Bar from *Police Academy*. He didn't appreciate the feedback.) Heath was a big kid and wasted no time establishing his spot near the top of the hierarchy. It isn't normal for a new guy to be the bully, but that's exactly what Heath did. He had a good eye for potential victims. He started with a few of the foreign kids and then moved on to bigger game. Before long almost everyone was scared of him.

I made it known to my table in the lunchroom that I was sick and tired of Heath. Word got back to him (because snitching to instigate a fight was acceptable) and suddenly I was obliged to fisticuffs. Heath couldn't let the challenge go unanswered. I sure as hell couldn't back down from my bluster. The bluster wasn't spontaneous. I saw in Heath a tough-talking blowhard who could easily be taken down. My classmates bought into his tough-guy shtick, but I had a read of that boy's soul. My suspicions were confirmed when he delayed the showdown.

"Carter Grocery," he told me. "Last day of school. I'll whoop your ass then."

I accepted the challenge. Heath was heavily favored to win.

I was driving to the meeting spot when it occurred to me out of nowhere: "That's funny. The mountain goes away down here."

I arrived to a large crowd. The clerk didn't seem concerned. He stood by the door and watched with a half-smile and a bottle of root beer. I parked and joined some friends.

"You ready for this, Jer?" one of them said.

"Goddamn right."

I lit a cigarette and watched each car as it pulled off the highway. They soon stopped coming and the crowd grew impatient. A few of the guys gave me dirty looks as if I had something to do with Heath's absence. When it became clear he wasn't coming, I finally felt afraid. Everyone wanted a fight and if they didn't get the one they came for, then they might have to settle for kicking me around.

"Let's go to his house," somebody said, thinking he was calling my bluff.

Then we realized that nobody knew where Heath lived. Half the grade was in that parking lot and not a one of us had been to his house. Heath's no-show would be an unsolved mystery until the beginning of our senior year. He was absent on the first day. We never saw him again.

I got some credit for showing up at Carter's, but nothing like the rep I was in line for by serving Heath a beatdown. I was more disappointed because I was looking forward to serving that beatdown. Heath had it coming and it didn't seem fair to me that he could walk away after causing so much trouble. It was an early life lesson, I suppose.

# 8

I didn't learn much of anything in school, not the formal stuff, anyhow. Most of my teachers were sanctimonious and mean-spirited, the type of people who pray before fucking somebody over. I was a so-so student and mama didn't care about my grades. She said all the right things—"no playin' until you do your homework"; "mind your teachers"; "you damn well better not come home just to use the bathroom"—but education wasn't valued in my household. Mama was just reciting what she thought a good parent is supposed to say.

I took on debt to go to Radford and never regretted the decision. Back then, tuition was on the cheaper side, not like now, where you have to be a robber baron to foot the bill. I didn't take much formal learning into college, but I had a good sense of how susceptible other people are to flimflam. You could get a guy to do some crazy things by flattering his vanity.

That's what we did to Slop Bucket, one of my friends in high school. Slop Bucket's real name was Henry, but nobody called him that, not even teachers and parents. Somebody gave him the name Slop Bucket in seventh grade and it stuck. Slop Bucket lived in one of those old foursquare houses next to downtown that must have looked beautiful when they were built. By the time of our generation, though, they were gloomy and rundown and filled with people who looked even more decrepit, people we used to call "grits" back in those days. Slop Bucket's parents were never around, and smacked out when they were, and so he and his five siblings were known to eat anything they could get their hands on. I once walked in on him and a brother squirting packets of Hardees ketchup into their mouths. We had fun over the years daring Slop Bucket to eat disgusting concoctions.

After a while, a willingness to swallow anything became his identity and he probably felt a lot of pressure to live up to his reputation. If he didn't, then he'd have to wait for a new reputation that might not be as good. Being Slop Bucket, a guy with friends and a claim to some kind of talent, however dubious, was better than being Henry, some random kid with shitty parents and not enough to eat. Slop Bucket wasn't an idiot, though. Nobody knew how it happened, because his siblings were dumb as stumps, but Slop Bucket was downright intelligent. He made good grades without studying. Math came easily to him and he got put in the advanced English classes while his friends, including me, went to the bonehead sections. Being known as smart still wasn't as good as being known for eating pizza smeared with refried beans.

Slop Bucket was part of the group I went with to Myrtle Beach for senior week. For some of my classmates, getting permission was a struggle, and some weren't allowed to go. A lot of kids got into trouble with the law during senior week. It was a dangerous scene for knuckleheaded teenagers. Mama knew nothing about senior week and I wouldn't have listened if she had prohibited me from going, anyway. Nowadays parents tag along as chaperones and the preppy kids stay in nice hotels and Airbnbs, but in my time senior week was more chaotic. We had no parental oversight and stayed in the long row of junky motels lining the Grand Strand.

Our place was called the Hurl Rock and it was trashier than the name made it sound. The whole point of senior week was to drink and get laid and my group, eight of us crammed into a single room, got right to it after dropping our bags—well, the first part of it, anyhow. I was fairly certain I'd get lucky once or twice during my eight days in Myrtle, but most of my friends would strike out, despite being in denial about it, and turn to drink as an antidote. I was on high alert for random violence.

When we opened the hooch, it felt anticlimactic. For months we talked about how glorious it would be in Myrtle, but in the moment we could have been in the high school parking lot for all the dullness of yet another drink-a-thon. We had beer bongs and hard liquor because getting fucked up made a man out of you and manhood depended on consumption. It felt the same no matter where it happened.

When Slop Bucket filled the bong with a can of Natural Light, one of our friends stopped him and suggested adding another. Slop Bucket, he declared, was wasting his talent with single cans of piss water. Slop Bucket shrugged his approval. Nobody asked Slop Bucket to put anything down his throat thinking he'd say no. He poured another can into the cylinder. Before he lifted the bong again, somebody else shouted for Slop Bucket to hold on. One of the boys appeared with a half-gallon of Everclear and dumped about six glugs into the bong. Slop Bucket didn't seem concerned.

By that point, a crowd had gathered, elbowing one another and snickering.

"Shit, that ain't strong enough, Slop Bucket," I said.

"Okay," he shrugged.

"Ay, who's got more liquor?" I yelled.

After some more snickering, somebody handed me a bottle of Nyquil. "That shit's got plentya alcohol in it," he said.

"I guess it'll do. Whaddya say, Slop Bucket?"

"Sure." If he was worried, it didn't show on his face.

"That crazy sonofabitch," somebody whooped.

I tipped the bottle and an inky glob floated near the top of the liquid. We chanted "Slop!" as he downed the kooky cocktail in a single motion.

Everything seemed normal. Slop Bucket didn't so much as flinch. The crowd broke up into little groups and kept on drinking. A yellowish blanket of cigarette smoke floated through the room like a stratus cloud. After a while, a voice rose above the din: "Where's Slop Bucket?" We looked around and couldn't find him.

"Hey boys!" somebody called from the balcony. "Get out here. You gotta see this."

We ran to the balcony and saw Slop Bucket stumbling along the beach, trying to chase a group of girls about a hundred yards away. The girls were moving slowly, but Slop Bucket couldn't catch up to them. In his mind, he was running. In reality, he was lurching side to side, yelling, "Hey! Hey you ladies! Wait up! I wanna talk to ya." He caught a few stares, but most everyone, including the girls, ignored him. Suddenly he stopped flailing and stood still, heaving from exertion. He kicked out a leg, spun around, and face-planted into the sand.

We roared with laughter and ran down to the beach to retrieve our friend, who was in no condition to stand and walk. We dragged him back to the room, carrying him up the stairs by his armpits and ankles so as not to whack his head.

"Is he dead?" somebody said after we tossed Slop Bucket onto the bed.

A few of us examined him at close range.

"Nah," I said. "Check it out. He's shiverin'."

They weren't shivers so much as convulsions, but Slop Bucket's nerves were still firing. It didn't occur to any of us to take him to the hospital. Maybe it did and we just didn't want to. I don't remember, exactly. I know that every now and again somebody would check to see that he was still breathing. He slept into that afternoon and then through the night, finally waking up past noon the next day. He sat up all of a sudden and said, "Goddamn I'm hungry."

We rushed to serve him whatever food was available, along with some stuff that probably didn't qualify as food. Slop Bucket enjoyed a week of admiration, although he didn't get laid.

Now, you might say that I was wrong to have spiked Slop Bucket's drink. It seems that way on the surface. In reality, though, I did it because I liked him. Every performer needs an audience. I might not have been able to put it that way at the time, but I understood the concept.

We ended up getting kicked out of the Hurl Rock two days early. The motel had a raggedy little pool on the beach side and a bunch of us were splashing around while our buddies threw cans of beer from the balcony. At least one boy would suffer what I now recognize as an undiagnosed concussion. In the middle of our game, the hotel owner's son walked out to the pool deck. He was Indian or Pakistani or something, around our age, maybe a college kid, and we'd already had a few run-ins with him. None of us liked his knit polo shirts and spiffy white tennis shoes—among other things I don't care to repeat at the moment.

He began bitching at us and I guess we'd consumed enough beer because before you know it we were surrounding him. All the kid needed to do was talk a little shit and we were ready to jump him. He talked shit and proved the theory correct. We didn't give him a vicious beating or anything, but there were enough shots to the face to make it clear we believed that the customer is always right. He ran off muttering about all the rednecks he has to deal with. About an hour later, a stocky bald security guard with a tufty little mustache showed up and removed us at gunpoint from the premises. Turns out that the owner is usually the one who's right. He has the cops on speed dial, after all.

Our almost-week in Myrtle Beach wasn't unusual. That's how things were. I didn't know anyone who made apple butter or listened to bluegrass. I knew kids with ugly nicknames and aberrant tendencies, kids who casually engaged in arson and property damage, kids who huffed gas and ate condiments for dinner. We were mean and uncaring and trying like hell to survive in a world that treated us with unvarnished contempt. We internalized that contempt and directed it at one another.

Missy was a goody-two-shoes, but she saw what I saw growing up. She knew what it was like. I didn't blame her for focusing on the rustic shit, but it was as alien to me as California beach culture. I reckon I had more in common with a typical street thug anywhere in the world than with a professional clog dancer. I sure as hell wasn't supposed to write the kind of stuff that would interest city boys like Rodrigo, but contrary to stereotype my upbringing in the mountains gave me plenty of know-how in the ways of modern life.

# 9

It was mostly by chance that I got started on a novel. It was looking like I'd be another Radford lifer with receding dreams of literary triumph when I got wind of a writers' retreat in Costa Rica. Well, it wasn't a writers' retreat, specifically, but a place that sounded mighty fine for writing.

At that point, I'd visited fewer than a dozen states and had never been out of the country. People of my station from Bluefield didn't travel. We crossed the state line a couple of times a week, but didn't get much further. Mama didn't have the money or curiosity. I was nearly forty and still hadn't been on an airplane.

I wouldn't have minded traveling, but it didn't often cross my mind. I suppose it wasn't something mama trained me to think about. When the department chair sent out a link about the place in Costa Rica, it caught my attention.

"Jerry," I told myself, "you're halfway to death and still ain't been anyplace interestin'. Get your sorry ass to Costa Rica and see if it can't inspire you."

I ended up with more inspiration that I ever imagined. The place in Costa Rica billed itself as a wellness retreat for artists (writers, painters, musicians, the whole shebang). It was on a hillside about twenty-five miles from San José, surrounded by dense tropical forest. Room and board were subsidized by some bigwig American, but the place still cost a pretty penny. Over the years I'd saved a nice little bundle and was happy to spend some of it. I didn't think I'd live into old age if I stayed at Radford, anyway.

I landed in San Jose and fell in love. We had a kid in our group growing up whose mom was from Central America. By eighth grade, it was obvious to everyone that he was gay, although he swore up and down that he was into girls. We tormented the poor guy. He took it because there was no other choice. If you wanted friends in Bluefield, then you had to deal with ridicule. We acted like it was all in good fun, but some of it could be vicious. Nobody was spared, but there were different levels depending on how close you were to normal. It didn't help this particular kid that his mom was the Spanish teacher. (Did anyone consider that poor bastard an Appalachian?) Once I got to Costa Rica, I paid for being such a slacker in her class. She used to tell me that I'm smart and that one day I'd regret not studying. I laughed her off. Speaking anything but a specific type of English was frowned upon in Bluefield.

I didn't begin my novel at the retreat, but being there eased my mind into all kinds of ideas. The place reminded me of Appalachia. The mountains were shaped differently, and the flora was practically from another planet, but the sense of being trapped by an emphatic landscape was exactly the same.

I loved the rain in Central America. It landed cold but smelled warm, like fog on a humid summer morning. I spent hours on the veranda listening to the din of birds from the jungle, taking in a breeze packed with the sweet odor of heliconia petals and palm fronds. I took long walks, sometimes drifting off the path. We had been warned not to wander too far from the property, but snakes and jaguars didn't frighten me. The place was too vibrant to feel ominous.

It was when I moved northward that my idea took shape. I headed to Nicaragua and fell in love again. The serenity of Costa Rica's countryside was replaced by Managua's urban chaos. I wandered the streets at dusk and returned to my hostel well after dark, coated in dusty sweat. I saw my first volcano and went boating on both of the country's enormous lakes. They were polluted like hell, but still some of the prettiest places I've ever seen.

Next was Honduras, which seemed even less in order than Nicaragua. By that point, I was communicating in halting Spanish–Señora Linares back at my old high school wouldn't have been proud, but she might have been less disgusted–and made my way around Tegucigalpa on foot, enjoying the hectic street action and, to my own shock, avoiding the special nightlife available to gringos. It was in Guatemala that I felt most grounded. I never wanted to leave. The country was a sensual wonder: the altitude, the old colonial architecture, the smell of decay and roasted corn. I spent many mornings feeding pigeons in the plaza of the main cathedral, an imposing stone building with a gothic vibe. In those moments I finally felt like the old man I was becoming. As in prior stops, I had nothing specific to do. I was just enjoying the sights and sounds of a different culture.

One day, on a tip from a fellow gringo, I visited an Indigenous village a few hours outside the capital. The gringo told me that you could buy killer fabrics and handicrafts for cheap. I felt an equal sense of calm and foreboding as the taxi I'd hired puttered along a narrow road with a steep drop-off at its edge. The surroundings were lush and misty. "Jesus Christ, Jerry," I kept thinking. "What the hell have you gotten yourself into?" I didn't know anyone. I didn't know a single word of any Indian language and still wasn't comfortable in Spanish. I didn't even know what language the people spoke where we were going.

The driver dropped me off at the edge of the village, terraced along a defoliated hillside with some modest fields behind it. I didn't know where to go and my driver had the look of a man about to nap. I stepped out of the car and slowly walked along the main road, taking in the surroundings. The village was peaceful but not picturesque. The houses were no more than tin shacks, most of them busted up. There were some stores along the street, but nothing that would attract tourists: a few cubbies promising ice-cold soda and probably lying about it. I caught some stares as I wandered around, but nobody seemed much interested in me. Eventually an elderly woman emerged from a fruit stall and spoke to me in English.

"You okay, Mister?"

"Um, yes, ma'am," I said slowly.

"What I can help you with?"

"Well, I'm just checkin' things out. Was hopin' maybe to find some sweaters." I made like I was putting on a shawl.

"Come," the old woman said, leading me down the street to a church. I wondered if she misunderstood me to mean I was looking for God.

She rushed past a tiny sanctum and into some kind of utility room, where four women were dyeing and spinning wool. I noticed a small pile of backpacks in the corner. As the women chatted, I sifted through the knitwork stacked against a wall. The stuff was nice. I liked the zigzagging color patterns. I saw a beanie—back in Bluefield we called them "toboggans"—that Missy would like: baby blue with braided ties and red inlays. I'd get her one if the women didn't try to fleece me. They didn't talk to me as I browsed. They didn't seem to register my presence at all.

A group of men came in. They varied in age. The oldest was probably in his early sixties and the youngest a teenager. They began stuffing the backpacks and then left. I stared at the backdoor they'd exited from. The guide noticed my curiosity and walked over to me.

"*El norte*," she said, pointing toward the sky.

The guy who tipped me off had been correct: the stuff was cheap by gringo standards and I went back to the city with a bagful of handicrafts.

I kept returning to the village. I learned that its residents speak K'iche' and feed themselves through collective farming. Warming temperatures were interfering with their harvests and so they turned to crafts and textiles. Tourists and wealthy Guatemalans loved all things Indigenous, so long as it didn't involve actual people. Many of the village's women, and some of the men, began reproducing traditional designs and objects to be sold at a high-end shop in the capital. The shop owner and various middlemen took most of the money. What made its way back to the villagers helped to alleviate lean years in the harvest.

Beyond climate change, the village's main challenge was emigration. Over half its men of working age had made the journey north. Some were deported, some got locked up, and some made it across the US border, where they fanned out to Los Angeles, Houston, Virginia, and hundreds of other places. The lucky ones who evaded capture and found steady work sent money back home, but life in the USA was expensive and even the successful ones had little to spare.

I came to know the woman who originally helped me as Doña Justina. Besides selling fruit, she organized the village's festivals and ceremonies. She organized everything, really, including the comings and goings of its population. The little bit of English she spoke came from working as a nanny for a US expat family in the capital, a job she began at age fourteen. Doña Justina had raised a passel of wealthy children. She was fluent in Spanish and even knew a bit of German. Whenever I visited, I immediately went to see her. Doing so wasn't simply a matter of respect. Without Doña Justina's blessing, I wouldn't be welcome in the village. Through her guidance, I became acquainted with some of villagers' stories and wanted to hear more.

So I begged my department's chair for a semester's leave. She said no at first, but I kept hammering on the university's diversity requirements. How am I supposed to learn about different cultures, I wanted to know, if you won't let me hang out in a foreign country? A place where every person is diverse? I can't get this kind of professional development on campus. The chair finally granted my request.

I borrowed two grand from Missy, who was thrilled by my initiative, and rented an apartment in La Reformita. It was dingy, but had a working bathroom, which is all I really needed. Soon I was making deliveries from the village to the city. I didn't take any money for the job. The villagers paid me in access, a more valuable currency. Over the next few months, I became half-competent in Spanish and picked up a handful of K'iche' phrases, enough to add some authenticity to the novel I was planning to write.

I'd say that I was inspired, but it was more than that. I felt like I was on a mission, doing something unstoppable, something great. Once back in Radford, I cut out the carousing and spent my spare time on the novel. I spent some work time on it, too. My students got higher grades than they deserved, on fewer assignments. I couldn't be bothered to mark the usual discourses about legalizing weed and outlawing abortion. They'd matriculate to the next level of classes with the same skillset no matter what I did. Nothing was more teachable than their perception of me. My evaluations were excellent. My course was a cakewalk and I could still fit into a pair of jeans.

I had dreaded returning to the United States. The entire time I was in Central America, I wondered why the hell anyone went north, where the weather is shitty and the best educated folks are also the biggest rubes. I wanted to grab people's shoulders before they made the dangerous trek and shout, "Stay, goddammit! It ain't what you expect!" I wanted to explain that up north they'd have no community, no traditions, no history, just endless pressure to work and shop, along with plenty of trouble from the police. But in reality I knew why they left. Their version of Guatemala and Honduras was different than mine. I was an outsider, a tourist, and I related to those places in ways that were completely foreign to the locals. Some of them would probably look at Bluefield and see it as a model of serenity. They wouldn't know the lowkey violence and the private miseries in the heart of so many households; they'd only see the friendly banter and the beautiful land. All I saw in Central America was a utopia of street life and rustic villages. But the poverty was everywhere. You can live your whole life in a suburb or small town and not see any suffering, even when it's right around the corner. You don't really have to train yourself to miss the obvious; it's built into the way we learn. The Good Samaritans on campus are blinder than anyone when it comes to seeing past a façade.

They say the grass isn't always greener on the other side, but that's bullshit. The grass is generally greener. That's why most of us like to travel. The problem is, if all you see is grass, then you're missing the dirt beneath it. There's no place like home, true, but there's also someplace always better.

And that's why I wanted to avoid Virginia.

As the novel progressed, I waited for the moment that I would run out of ideas, a moment I'd experienced hundreds of times before. Some part of my subconscious would decide that I have fuck-all to say, or that I was saying nothing useful, and then my entire mind would shut down. This time it didn't happen. The fear stayed with me until I finished the last paragraph. Only after I dotted the final sentence did I feel a sense of accomplishment.

The feeling didn't last. I had no idea what to do after the novel was complete. I could've devoted more time to teaching and really give it all for my students. I could've returned to the party circuit and made the best of a boring town. I ended up smoking a lot of weed and cigarettes on my back porch, wondering what the heck to do with my life.

You see, the publishing process wasn't easy. It was an all-out disaster, as far as I'm concerned. I generally understood how the system works, but didn't have a single contact. No agents. No peers. No editors. I'd never written for literary magazines. I couldn't hit up colleagues for a favor because nobody at Radford was accomplished enough to have connections. I was starting from scratch in an industry that requires networking.

I spent a week writing a cover letter and a precis for the novel. I can't say if they were any good, but feel like I more or less approximated the examples I found online. I came to suspect that quality had little to do with it. More people write than read. It feels that way, anyhow. Whatever the case, I didn't stand a chance with blind queries. All the rejection notes sounded exactly the same. I preferred the agents who didn't bother to respond. Ignoring me seemed more tactful than sending a fake-polite letter.

I got so desperate that I ponied up for a few of those contests you have to pay to enter. The only thing that got me was a bruised ego.

So I headed off to that year's AWP conference. I'm not sure how to best describe AWP. I suppose you could say it's the big shindig for creative writers. It's where all the MFA programs send their people. The writing mecca for people with little imagination. Most everyone has some kind of university affiliation. People who earn a living as writers, without teaching, don't need to show up, so they have to be lured with prime speaking gigs and honoraria. A bunch of publishers show up, too, in rows of collapsible booths lined up like an upscale flea market. That year the convention was in DC, four hours from Radford, so I only needed to spring for a room and food, which I could do on the cheap. Even at the special convention rate, rooms at the Marriott Wardman Park and nearby Omni, were out of my range. I found a Days Inn a few metro stops up from the Marriott and booked on the veterans' discount. (Once they hear me talk, front desk clerks never ask to see military ID. They simply thank me for my service.)

On the first day, I climbed the steep hill up to the Marriott and went immediately to the book expo. I had no intention of attending the panels. The booths were stuffed into an enormous underground room with dubious ventilation. It smelled like an isolated library stack where snickering students sneak off for oral sex. After getting my bearings, I approached a well-known independent press. The woman behind the table looked fresh out of college. She sported oversized glasses with dark red frames and wore a thick smudge of rouge beneath her cheekbones to match the look. I glanced up to see her smiling at me.

"Hello there," I said, returning the smile.

"Is there anything I can help you with?"

I tried to read her nametag without being too obvious about it. I needed to know if this person had any real standing at the press or if she was just an intern. All I could make out was Madeleine Some-Such with the name of the press beneath it.

"Oh, I'm just a big fan. Wanna find some'n amazin' to read. Whaddya suggest?"

"Our entire spring list is amazing."

"Good," I thought to myself. "She ain't just an intern."

Out loud I said, "I'm more into fiction than anything."

"I can't entice you to give some poetry a try?" She spread her hands above a section of the table as if she were one of Barker's Beauties.

"I reckon I could give it a try."

"That's an interesting accent. Where are you from?"

"Virginia."

"No kidding? Same here."

I didn't have the heart to tell her that we came from the same state only in name. In reality, nothing but some legal mumbo-jumbo tied me to anyone from up north. Her Virginia and mine were entirely different hemispheres. But a civilized man, I reminded myself, seeks to overcome differences.

"I'm Maddy," she said, extending her hand.

"Jerry," I said with a slight bow. "Whatcha do here, Maddy?"

"I'm an acquisitions editor."

Jackpot.

We kept on chatting and I knew she was enjoying it. I'm a decent-looking guy: tall and thin with broad shoulders and thick graying stubble on my chin, a scrubby complement to my straight brown hair, which I wear between ear- and shoulder-length. There's not a ton of them, but a certain kind of educated woman—a fancy woman, we'd call them back in Bluefield—has a thing for redneck types as long as they don't look poor. And I could tell that Maddy came from money the moment I set eyes on her. It's practically required to get a paying job in any artistic industry.

My assumption about her age turned out to be wrong. Maddy wasn't fresh out of college. She was in her early thirties. I had to remind myself that people with office jobs don't age like people who do real work. I was proof enough. I looked at least ten years younger than Ronnie when he was my current age.

Other people kept wandering into the booth, but Maddy mostly ignored them. She finally had to turn me away because of some meetings, but we made plans to get together at the hotel bar in the evening. I hightailed it back to the Days Inn for a nap and shower. I took a taxi back to the Marriott because I didn't want to smell like the metro.

The bar was packed–a real jackpot for conference hotels–and I weaved through groups of people in loud conversation. Everything about them was overdone: the studiously casual clothes; the pathological need to be heard; the bogus laughter. I kept walking but the maze of drunken blabbermouths seemed endless. I finally found my way to a less crowded seating area and found Maddy in an armchair, talking to some guy in a cardigan. I walked up to them and interrupted the conversation. The guy glared at me, but Maddy had already turned her back to him.

We had a nice conversation over mixed drinks, leaning in to one another because of the noise. Whenever I brought up publishing, Maddy brushed it off without breaking stride. She had this amazing ability to repel anything that might involve work. I respected the sentiment, but needed her to make an exception on my behalf. Otherwise, everything was going well. She told me I have a great eye for literature. She loved my opinions about various writers. But she didn't give two shits about my own writing.

Well, I'm not a picky man and mama always told me to take what I can get, so I resigned myself to a different kind of working relationship with Maddy. After enough tequila, she wasn't coy about it.

"Let's go to your room," she whispered, glassy-eyed.

"Well, darlin'," I said, remembering my hotel situation, "I'm over at the Omni and I don't reckon it's a good idea for us to try and cross the street in our condition."

She considered the point.

"Much easier to just go upstairs," I added.

"Come on," she said.

I'll tell you what: sometimes you just can't judge a person's intimate habits by their appearance. Maddy might have looked bookish, but she behaved more like a fictional character. There's no point in being crass, so let me just say that Maddy had me too tired to take trains or taxis. Luckily, she didn't kick me out when it was time to sleep.

She didn't seem embarrassed in the morning, either. We played around for a good little while before she nudged me out.

"It's been fun, Jerry, but I have to get ready now."

"That's a goddamn shame."

"Yeah. But, well, you know."

"Quick question before I go."

"Sure."

"What would I have to do to get my novel into your hands?"

She glared at me with unbridled contempt. "Bye, Jerry."

# 10

I was slick enough to charm Maddie, but too stupid to impress her. Clothes, hairstyle, expression, attitude . . . they were all like a text already imprinted onto my brain, available for easy interpretation. I was always good at that kind of literary criticism. These days I think a lot about that skill, if you can call it a skill. I don't really know what it is—garden-variety perceptiveness, I suppose—but I've decided that it never helped me. Not really. I mean, it did some short-term good every now and again. On the whole, though, figuring out how to get over on other people only opens you up to getting got. Real success—the kind that leads to fame and money—requires something more than cleverness. You have to be ruthless, too. It's a tall order. I always considered myself up to the task—my upbringing had trained me for it—but only after my confrontation with Rodrigo did I realize that it just wasn't in me. My meanness didn't have any ambition. I didn't understand the right way to use violence. My arrogance was actually unacknowledged humility.

If I had more than garden-variety perceptiveness, then maybe I would have recognized my limitations earlier. Looking back on my life, I can find a bunch of examples I didn't recognize in the moment.

One stands out from when I was in college. I'm not sure which year, but I was an undergrad. It must have been the start of sophomore year because some of the boys from Bluefield met up with me and a few dormmates. I remember Jolly being there and I never saw Jolly past a year or thereabouts after high school graduation.

I don't know why he was called Jolly. He wasn't jollier than anyone else. It was probably a nickname he caught when he was a toddler or something. Parents are always giving out nicknames that don't make sense to other people.

Jolly had pasty skin and soft orange hair with a middle part. I always thought his head looked like a rotten tooth. He drove a hand-me-down clunker from his parents with an 8-track player and a tailpipe that smacked the road whenever he hit a pothole. He was driving the same clunker when he rolled up to the New River with a contingent of Bluefield boys. I can't remember what the place was called, but you drove a few miles down a country road outside of Blacksburg lined with small farms and dingy houses until arriving at a wide and shallow section of the river. The holler you went down was called McCoy, but it's a different clan of McCoys than the one you're thinking of. On the riverbank was a parking lot and a shack that rented out innertubes. The place attracted a mixture of locals and college students, who mostly kept out of each other's way.

I remember Jolly being around that day because he was the one who noticed the little boy floating down the river.

I greeted my old friends and introduced them to my new ones. We were milling around and shooting the shit when Jolly asked me to toss him a pack of smokes from his car. I leaned into the window and opened the glove box. Inside were two packs of Camel Wides, a little stack of paperwork, some balled-up tissues, and a can of mace.

It was obvious what needed to be done.

I called Jolly over.

"Whaddya want?" he shouted.

"You gotta see this, man."

"What is it?"

"I can't describe it. It's fuckin' nuts. Hurry."

As Jolly approached, I held my breath and sprayed a bunch of mace into the front of the car.

"Look inside," I said when Jolly arrived.

He stuck his head into the car.

"I don't see nothin'," he said before going into a coughing fit.

I tried to suppress my laughter. Jolly stumbled out of the car, screaming, and rolled around the ground with his palms pressed against his eyes. The rest of the guys wandered over to see if there was a problem. I explained the situation. The Bluefield contingent cracked up. After the sting wore down a bit, Jolly stared at us with puffy red eyes and cussed us up one side of the lot and down the other. We helped him to his feet and carried on with the teasing. The guys from Radford watched in silence.

We rented our innertubes and plopped into the river. The water was warm that time of year so it wasn't any problem to get wet. It was a nice scene: we bunched together, bouncing around like bumper cars, with the little cooler tubes trailing behind. (You were supposed to put empty cans back into the cooler, but most everyone tossed them into the water.) Every so often we had to lift our asses to keep from getting stuck on a rock. Otherwise we floated along, looking up at the steep green hillsides lining the river. It never took long for somebody to make a pointless comment.

Some small rapids around a mile or so downriver were supposed to be the highlight of the journey. People sunned themselves on the huge rocks sticking out of the water. After the rapids, the water turned into a rusty color and became much deeper. Tubers exited on a muddy beach and waited for a rickety school bus to take them back to the lot.

That's where we were sitting, soaked and half-drunk, when Jolly nudged me with his elbow.

"Hey, that little guy just went over the rapids without a tube."

People did that sometimes—jumped out of the inner-tube and rode the rapids in a diving position. I'd never seen a kid do it, though. I caught sight of the boy when he was below the rocks. The current began carrying him down the river.

"That's nuts," I mumbled, undisturbed.

"Dumb motherfuckers," Jolly said, wringing out his sopping red hair.

He must have been referring to the parents, who were nowhere in sight, or else indifferent. I turned my attention back to the boy and realized that something was wrong. It seemed like he was screaming, or trying to scream, but his voice was swallowed by the noise of the river. He bobbed along and it looked like he was keeping his head above water. Something didn't feel right to me, though.

"Should I go get'm?" I said.

"Nah, he's fine. His folks need to get their heads out their asses is all."

I scanned the rocks and saw no commotion, just the usual groups of people slamming beer in the midday sun. The boy's head still appeared to be above water, but he had quit trying to scream. I decided to check it out.

When I reached the boy, I immediately saw that he wasn't right. He coughed and gurgled when trying to speak. I hooked my wrist underneath his armpit and told him to squeeze. He could barely muster the energy.

I'm a decent swimmer, but let me tell you: it's hard as all hell trying to keep a person's head above water when he's gone limp, even a little fellow. Well, I managed to do it, but only by repeatedly going under myself. By the time we got to the beach, I was exhausted. The boy looked okay. A bunch of people gathered around him, asking if he needed anything.

"He needs some goddamn parents," I thought as I lay in the mud, heaving.

Right on cue, a man and a woman–some real hillbilly sons of bitches–started running across the rocks, yelling after the kid.

"Petey! Petey! Where are you? What happened?"

They found a good spot to jump into the water and swam over to the crowd.

"Mama," little Petey gurgled when she reached him, clamoring on about what had happened.

The father tried to explain the lapse to the crowd. "He likes swimmin' in a little pool up there. S'pose the current took'm for a ride."

I was still stretched out on the bank and spat in disgust. It wasn't an accident, not in the sense that the parents were making it out to be. They were boozing and showing out for their neighbors and nobody noticed the boy. It didn't matter if the boy meant to go down the rapids. They should have been watching him.

That's how I felt about it.

They must have secretly felt the same way because soon as they discovered that I was the one who pulled their son out of the river they came over and stared down at me. I didn't like the view, so I struggled to my feet, expecting a show of gratitude. What I got instead was a reaming.

That's how I knew they felt guilty. They laid into me about touching their child without permission, about butting into other people's business, about making a big show of nothing. It almost made me respect them more. Not everyone's willing to make such an obvious confession.

I was fixing to let them get it off their chest and then go on my way, but they wouldn't shut up so I ran out of patience. I got in the dad's face and clenched up. Normally the bystanders would at least pretend to intervene. "C'mon, gentlemen, no need for any of that." But they let this one ride. Everyone understood that the situation was serious and one of us needed to catch an ass-kicking.

I didn't know whose side the crowd was on and didn't care. I belted the guy in his belly and made quick work of him afterward. With one uppercut, he was on the ground, streams of blood rolling down his cheeks and chin.

I'll tell you, though, I was mad. Normally you give a guy a few punches and you feel fine afterward. You might not even remember why you were so pissed off in the first place. But belting that sloppy bastard only made me madder. I don't know what had come over me. Maybe it was the sense that for once I was fighting for a good reason. Or maybe I didn't like being blamed for the parents' negligence. I don't know. I wasn't ready to stop, that's all.

I walked to the edge of the woods and found a thick branch. I heard a few gasps as I walked back to the guy. His wife was fussing over him, but scampered away when she saw me. I whacked the son of a bitch a good one on his thigh and then popped him on the head with a bit less force.

By then the child was wailing and my friends were beginning to get antsy.

"Hey, dude, that's enough," one of my dormmates said, pulling me away by the arm. I glared at him, shook my arm free, and headed up the path to the road. I began walking with the stick still in hand. Everyone was too scared to approach me, so a small group followed behind. A minute later the bus scooped us and drove us back to the lot, where the police had just arrived.

# PART II

# 1

It was by chance that I discovered Rodrigo Suarez. I was at the Barnes & Noble in Christiansburg when I saw a stack of books on a display table. For a second, I thought I was hallucinating. The book was called *Coyote Road*, the exact title of my unpublished novel. The bookstore was clearly making it a priority. The copies piled atop one another suggested that it was an important book, something a lot of people would be reading–or should be, anyway. You didn't want to miss out. The cover showed a group of migrants, dark and serious, huddled together in the back of a pickup truck, a dusty, sunny landscape surrounding them. The cover was splashed with blurbs from famous authors and critics. The whole thing was glossy and colorful and completely eye-catching. It was an expensive design.

I was annoyed but took it in stride. So some asshole had used the title before I got a chance. It wasn't a huge deal. Whatever. A title is easy to change. Still, it was a pretty big coincidence.

Just like it was a big coincidence that the book seemed to have the same theme: a group of people trying to illegally cross from Mexico to the United States. That was some real shitty luck. What were the chances? Against my better judgment, I picked up a copy—about the same size mine would be if it ever got published—and opened it to the first page. I almost fell straight to the floor. I was reading the novel I had written, word for word.

# 2

I spent a long time with Rodrigo Suarez's opus that afternoon. At first, I was confused. I knew what I was seeing, but it didn't seem real. Maybe the coincidences extended to an identical first paragraph, I told myself. It wasn't technically impossible, right?

See, the shock had made me delusional. Part of my mind knew exactly what was going on, and another part of it didn't know how to process the situation. The delusion dropped away when I kept skimming the book. No matter what page I opened it to, I saw my own words, verbatim. It wasn't some kinda-sorta plagiarism, the borderline stuff that people debate on the internet. That fucker stole my novel whole cloth.

I had read the history. I had done the research. I had traveled to another part of the world. I had spent countless nights typing and deleting flaccid adjectives until the edge of dawn. Instead of the pleasure of seeing my work in print, I was left with the cold, crass reality of having been picked clean like a squirrel carcass.

I had everything but an authentic cultural identity. I wasn't whatever the pantsuit and sportscoat set would consider authentic or exotic. I had no hyphen, no X in my identity. Hell, I wasn't just a white male, the absolute worst combination for writing about anybody other than white males; I was a white male from the middle of nowhere, a regular avatar of Trump Country. I don't know what made me ever think I could write about Guatemalans. I guess I believed all the crap about art transcending borders, as if art has some magical ability to float above the humans who create it.

Be that as it may, I did the work, I can promise you that. This clown Rodrigo may have sounded legit, but he was a fraud and I damn sure wasn't going to let him get away with it.

I flipped to the back page and checked out his photo and bio. His face almost made me vomit. He had that smug, cocksure expression that nearly all authors wear in their headshots. They try to look profound to the point of being dangerous. Those photos practically scream, "Avoid me if you're smart. I'm deeply unpleasant and complain about everything." He'd been gussied up pretty good: his straight brown hair had a side part and was just long enough to drop over the top of his ears. His eyes were dark, more aloof than steely. His bio didn't give me much to go on: "Rodrigo Suarez is a descendant of the K'iche' people of Guatemala, where his mother was born and raised. He is a queer multimedia artist and earned his MFA from the University of Michigan. He lives in New York City. *Coyote Road* is his first novel." I read the bio a few times. Something about it was off. To begin with, he didn't look very Indian to me. Not like any of the ones I saw in Guatemala, that's for sure.

I didn't learn until later—the hard way—that you're not supposed to judge a person's Indianness by his appearance. You'll get blasted for doing race science. All right, whatever, fair enough, but it didn't change the fact that Rodrigo looked like a mashup of every Yankee prick getting drunk at the AWP convention. He didn't look *anything*. He was just a guy. Like a human manifestation of neutrality or something.

After a while, I put my finger on a few of the oddities in the bio. Rodrigo didn't say anything about a father. That wasn't weird on its own, I suppose, but he did mention his mother. Who talks about their parents in an author bio? I couldn't imagine saying, "Turley's mom was standard Southern Appalachian white trash with terrible taste in men." The other thing I noticed is that Rodrigo didn't mention any professional accomplishments, just some random biographical stuff.

I had found an armchair in the stacks and was camped out for a few hours, perusing the book and downing caffeine. I was on my fifth espresso when my stomach gave out. I put the book under my armpit and trotted to the back of the store, ignoring the sign warning against taking inventory into the bathroom as I blew into a stall. I couldn't stop flipping to random pages. It was bizarre, seeing my own work presented to me as another person's.

How did it happen? How *could* it happen? I sweated and strained and felt even more tortured by the impossibility of those questions. After finishing, I left the book on top of the toilet tank and rushed home.

I spent the next five hours on Google. There were like twenty tabs open on my computer. Rodrigo was everywhere and yet he was bizarrely absent. It's hard to explain. He had a million things to say about his life, but if you paid attention the details were vague. Rodrigo could spit out tons of information without actually telling you anything. He had a huge following and was a darling of the social justice crowd. You could find him in all kinds of online publications and in a decent amount of traditional media. Just not as an author. Rodrigo had no record of publication. I checked academic and literary journals. I searched for old blogs. I even looked for a Tumblr. Rodrigo had published the novel, which was a smash hit. Otherwise, he was all hype.

His family situation was no clearer. It's not that Rodrigo was shy to discuss his parents. To the contrary, he never shut up about his personal life. His entire persona *was* his private life. You can't trust a motherfucker who constantly brings up tragedy as if it's a coupon to be redeemed for a cheaper transaction. Those motherfuckers and the other kind who are always in a squabble or some other kind of drama. You know the kind: always screaming on somebody, always guilting people into giving them money, always in a huff about a whole bunch of nothing. This kind of motherfucker is either lying or in serious need of attention—or both, in a lot of cases.

That was Rodrigo, a real shit-for-brains smart enough to con a whole bunch of people who were even dumber. He sure as hell wasn't smart enough to have written the words in the book with his name on the cover.

He didn't mention his father in his author bio because his father was a stranger. That's the story he told, over and over again. The father was supposedly a Catalonian tourist to Guatemala who had impregnated his mother in a secret affair opposed by both families. The father either didn't know about the pregnancy before he fled or he fled because he found out about the pregnancy. Whatever the case, he was a source of great disgrace to Rodrigo, what with his colonizer's blood and abusive personality. Rodrigo often complained about the ghastly European DNA this man had bequeathed on him.

His mother was a godly creature. She had died some years back, leaving Rodrigo adrift in a harsh and scary world. He had to deal with poverty, with contempt, with hunger, with microaggressions. He didn't spend a day in college without suffering this or that indignity from some heartless settler. His mother's spirit sustained him. He had to endure in order to honor her memory. It made no sense that she ever would have gotten with his father. She was quiet and kind, which made me think that Rodrigo inherited his father's personality. Rodrigo assumed that his mother was victim of the terrible sexual politics of colonization. It wasn't an equitable relationship. It wasn't even consensual, not with the uneven power dynamics. His father was basically a rapist.

K'iche' society is matrilineal, so Rodrigo fully claimed his mother's blood. She had no name. She was simply Mother, distinct and universal.

There wasn't much else to find out about the guy. He was famous now, not just as a writer but as the kind of person reporters and activists seek out for opinions. He was a thought-leader. I tried to comfort myself with a bit of logic: Rodrigo wasn't a thought-leader, per se. I was. It was my work that had stirred the masses. It was my work that had become a bestseller.

Then I got real: I was nothing but a two-bit hillbilly with questionable ethics and a future of infinite loneliness.

# 3

What to do? I had no earthly idea. Here's the thing: I never really had trouble making a good plan. I could implement a plan, too. I was never held back by gray areas. Unpleasant stuff sometimes needed to be done and so you bucked the fuck up and did it. That's how I was raised. My entire community instilled that attitude. I can't count the number of times that Ronnie fed me the line.

The community couldn't have prepared me for Rodrigo, though. Rodrigo didn't make any sense. Rodrigo had alien habits. Rodrigo talked funny. Most of all, Rodrigo wasn't accessible. He was entirely a creation of the internet and didn't seem to have a presence in the actual world.

I was determined to come up with a plan, though. No way I was going to let that donkey get rich off my work, but I was wise enough to not be hasty. I wouldn't have minded inflicting pain on Rodrigo, but the most important goal was to expose him as a fraud and get credit for my work. In order to do that, I needed to know what happened. How did he get hold of my manuscript? It was impossible. Even if he had stolen it from a submissions pile, the timeline didn't match up. Rodrigo hadn't pilfered an earlier version of my book. He had published the latest draft, with revisions I'd made within the past year.

It didn't make a lick of sense. Could he have stolen it from the cloud or whatever? I knew hardly anything about technology, but it didn't seem realistic. I always saved documents directly onto my hard drive. I think. Did he put some kind of trojan horse into my computer? But how in the world would he have known about me or my novel?

I went back to his social media and YouTube videos. He had that same generic look: slightly swarthy in a certain light, with sort of thin eyes, but you couldn't see the Indian in him unless you were looking for it—and even then you had to strain. He was a textbook coastal activist/intellectual type, with that same contemptuous expression and irregular cadence they all use to show people that they're Very Serious. Buh-dum-dum in the last three syllables of every sentence. Total headcase shit. Like sticking a flag on your tongue with the seal of an NGO imprinted on it.

Rodrigo didn't seem real. That was the problem. I needed a more legible enemy. He was a new media creation, but one highly attuned to the long American tradition of customer service. I didn't know what to do about him. But I damn sure intended to do something.

# 4

It was the beginning of the semester and the summer heat still hadn't cleared out of Radford. My hair was matted beneath a Steelers cap as I walked across campus to see Missy. We were both assigned to buildings that didn't exist when we were students. All the apartments I lived in had been torn down. Even an outpost in the sticks understood the importance of progress.

Missy was director of Appalachian Studies and I rarely saw her in the building that housed English. She kept busy teaching graduate seminars, doing community outreach, organizing conferences and field trips, and promoting her Center. Missy was a hard worker. She never explained her discipline in a way I could understand, but if the powers-that-be insisted on having an Appalachian Center then she was the best person to lead it.

I stuck my head in her doorway and waited for her to look up from her computer. When she saw me, she gasped and put her hands to her chest.

"Jesus, you scared me near to death, Jerrah!" I gave her a half-smile. "Well, c'mon," she said, waving me in.

I took out my wallet and handed her two bills. I was paying her back in monthly increments for the cash she'd fronted me to stay in Central America. It was always a bit awkward because Missy didn't like to think of herself as a loan shark. Taking cash made her feel undignified. I found her hang-ups amusing. She didn't charge interest and she wouldn't have said a word if I didn't return a nickel of her money. If I had a debtor into me for two large, then I'd for sure put points on the money, with a penalty for being late.

She quickly stuffed the bills into her purse and said, "Ain't you gonna sit down?" Her accent had grown heavier over the years.

I shrugged and took one of the seats across from her. I didn't have much to say, so I glanced absently at Missy's bookshelves and the bric-a-brac lining the windowsill behind her: wooden bowls, clay figurines, leathercraft, that kind of stuff. I knew she was waiting for me to talk, so I asked how she was doing.

"I'm fine," she said. "But some'n ain't right about you, Jerrah."

"Whaddya mean?" I tried not to sound defensive. I was genuinely curious.

"You seem like you're on cloud nine. Is some'n the matter?"

"Nah. Just tryin' to survive this heat."

"Nuh uh," she said, shaking her head. "It's some'n more."

"You're imaginin' things again, Missy."

It was a needlessly harsh line. Over the years, I said it as a joke and Missy pretended to receive it as a joke, but

I think deep down it hurt her feelings. The line made reference to the time in grad school that our cohort smoked some skunk I'd gotten hold of from a connection in Roanoke and Missy suffered mild hallucinations. The rest of the year we joked on her about the big-headed elves she claimed to have seen. But I was only partly joking. Missy had a habit of seeing things as she wanted them to be rather than as they were.

"If you say so," she shrugged.

I was ready to leave, but Missy would have thought it rude for me to hand her money and then go without a proper amount of chitchat. I considered asking her about Rodrigo, without mentioning his theft, just to see how familiar he was to the reading public. I decided against it because I couldn't bear the thought of other people conning Missy. My hesitation put into focus the difficulty I was facing.

"How's your family?" I said.

She talked for a few moments about the vacation she took with her parents to Asheville. They had gone hiking in the Smokies, toured the Biltmore, and eaten at the neatest little Indian restaurant. It was a street food concept, she explained. I smiled and nodded. Her parents had never eaten anything like that, she continued. They loved it. I'm sure they did, I replied. I was hoping that Missy would talk herself out. I didn't care about Asheville. I visited the Biltmore once. I remember thinking that somebody ought to bulldoze that overrated shitbox. I never got into the romance of these grand houses in the mountains. There are more of them than you'd think. Even a dump like Bramwell, deep in the hills of McDowell County, was once known as a bastion of millionaires. Before everyone fled the dying coal economy, and the town had enough students to fill a few classrooms, the Bramwell High School nickname was Millionaires. Those palaces account for the tin cans people live in everywhere else. I saw no reason to celebrate them. Most were butt-ugly, anyway. If there hadn't been so many people around, I would have happily left a steaming log next to the posies in the Biltmore Garden.

Missy interrupted my daydreaming. "Are you even listenin' to me?"

"Of course. You was talkin' about all the microbrews in Asheville."

"No, I was sayin' that you seem distant."

She had me there. "Now, Missy, don't go around worryin' about me. Everthing's fine."

I said goodbye and darted before she could start on a new topic. Missy's worrying is exactly why I couldn't confide in her about the thing with Rodrigo. If she believed me—and I doubted that even someone as earnest as Missy would buy my story—then she'd be up in arms and I'd have to manage her response in addition to whatever I intended to do about Rodrigo. I learned a long time ago that an indignant Missy ain't nothing to sneeze at.

I headed over to the 7-Eleven to buy a Gatorade. It was crowded with frat boys hauling out cases of beer for the weekend. I grabbed a bottle of Glacier Cherry and sat at a stool next to the checkout counter. I sipped the drink while waiting for Sam to finish up with some customers. Sam had worked at 7-Eleven since I was a student. He was an old man now—he seemed like an old man to me then—who always wore flannel and a John Deere baseball cap. Sam acknowledged me with a nod and steadily handled transactions. When the last customer had checked out, he leaned against the counter. "Wha's goin' on, Jer?"

"Eh, a whole lotta nothin'. Just tryin' to keep out of this heat."

"Yep." Even with his cap, it didn't seem like Sam was doing a good job of it. The skin around his white mustache was leathery with deep diagonal wrinkles. "Whatchu up to?"

"Gotta go teach class in a bit. Thought I'd burn some time in the meanwhile."

"Yep."

"Anything interestin' goin' on?" Sam was my go-to for town gossip.

"The president come in here the other day. Bought a Kit-Kat."

"You don't say. I took her for an Almond Joy kind of gal."

"Me too."

We sat in silence for a few moments.

"Let me ask you some'n, Sam. What would you do if you caught someone stealin' from you?"

"Well, it depends. From me or the store?"

"Let's say the store."

"These days, I'd ask 'em to have a seat while I call the cops. If they don't listen, maybe I call the cops or maybe pretend I didn't see nothin'. I'm too old to be chasin' down these youngsters. Can't tell what some of 'em might do, anyhow."

"What about from you?"

"I'd get my hind end in gear and shoot the sonofabitch."

"That's what I figured. Take it easy, Sam."

I tossed the empty Gatorade bottle into the bin at Sam's feet and headed back to my office. I shared it with two other instructors, but they weren't in. I decided to call an old buddy, Terry. He answered on the first ring. "Wha's goin' on, partner?"

"This'n'that. Just checkin' in. You at work?"

"Sure am." For Terry, "work" was a loose concept. He could have been delivering pizzas or pushing oxy. If he was off the couch, then he was working, even if he wasn't getting paid.

I didn't ask what kind of work he was doing. "Whatchu into this weekend?"

"I'm headed to the game tonight. Might fish on Saturday. You comin' in?"

He was referring to the Graham-Beaver game, a big deal in Bluefield. Every year, the high school on the Virginia side, Graham, played the high school on the West Virginia side, Bluefield (nicknamed the Beavers), and the entire town turned up for the game. The stadium was emptier by the year.

Speaking of, it's an old concrete junkpile called Mitchell Stadium. People like to say that the state line runs right through the length of the field, but that's a myth. The entire stadium is in West Virginia, but you can hock a loogie across the border from the top bleacher. The home side, which the Virginians sit on for the annual game, was half-built into a blasted-out hillside and when I was a tween I used to play behind the stands with my friends. There was a little-known concession stall back there and you could hike to the top of the hill and look down on the stadium. It was a steep and slippery ridge, but as far as I know nobody ever fell to their death. I don't remember any adults telling us to get down, either.

I have nice memories of the game. Anytime I want, I can cut through the clutter in my brain and conjure the scent of hot chocolate in the brisk autumn air, the excited buzz of townsfolk acting like high school kids, the rhythmic clatter of snare drums and trombones. Students had their own section and we spent two hours flirting and cussing and strutting like little billy badasses. The more adventurous kids would walk to the other side at the risk of getting jumped. There were at least three fights every year. The cops sometimes waited for a winner before breaking them up.

Terry was going to the game because he still lived in Bluefield and that's what you do if you live in Bluefield. He was one of the few people I kept in contact with even though I was only an hour away. I skipped both the ten- and twenty-year reunions, held at the Graham-Beaver game, and didn't regret it after getting updates from Terry: "Larry got drunk, hit on Brian's wife; Brian knocked him clean out"; "partied at Heather's house after the game; she took off her shirt again"; "Jimmy's in real estate now; Eric's in jail."

I didn't have anything good to share about my life. Being a professor at Radford–my old classmates didn't know the difference between faculty and instructional staff–wasn't anything to be ashamed of, but that's not how I thought of myself. I was a novelist. But it's goddamn hard to call yourself that in front of other people when you haven't published anything. The first thing they'll want to know is what your book is called. When you tell them you're still working on it, they reckon you're either full of shit or a failure.

I still hung out with Terry because we go way back and he's one of the few people I can trust to keep his mouth shut. Terry isn't exactly what you'd describe as a good person, but he's a good man. He doesn't snitch, he doesn't trust cops, and he doesn't chicken out. It's good to have someone like him on your side. I figured I might need his help with the Rodrigo situation.

I always thought Terry was destined for something better than a small-town hood. He's a bright guy, though he did poorly in school. I'm not just talking streetwise, either; he could have made good grades if he gave half a damn. I guess he didn't have the right motivation. Terry came up in West Graham, like me, and there wasn't much of an emphasis on education. Our folks banged on about work. The kids from nicer neighborhoods were nerdy or whatever, but being a nerd didn't fly on my side of town. We lacked good homes, proper nutrition, all that stuff, so we spent more time forging a little society of the unattended. Having a run of the streets was great, but it had drawbacks that would follow us all the way into adulthood.

Terry channeled his intelligence into street life. He could outwit anyone who wanted to whip him and he could whip anyone who to tried to outwit him. When we were in eighth grade, a huge guy named Bobby Keene, who had been held back at least twice, terrorized our class. Bobby was denser than a thundercloud, but that wasn't the main problem; he was also large, even for somebody close to being a legal adult, and mean to boot. Bobby would come up with cockamamie reasons to beat his unfortunate target to a pulp. In his mind, he wasn't a bully; he was just punishing sinners.

And so when he declared that Slop Bucket had flirted with his girlfriend, we knew that Slop Bucket was due for a whooping. The girlfriend, Becky, was one of the grittiest females in school, somebody even pubescent boys considered unfuckable. Not that we would have believed Bobby, anyway. Slop Bucket was too goofy to hit on anyone unless he'd bonged some Nyquil.

When the time came for Bobby to defend Becky's honor, we tried to dissuade him by forming a wall around Slop Bucket, but he busted through it and landed a haymaker before anyone could stop him. Slop Bucket hit the ground and Bobby went on his way, glaring at the crowd in case anyone thought to challenge him. We gathered in a circle around Slop Bucket and watched in awe as a knot swelled up just below his eye until it was the size of a ping-pong ball. It started red and then slowly turned purple. Slop Bucket stayed on the grass, chin against chest, breathing heavily. I finally snapped into action.

"You okay, Slop Bucket?"

He didn't respond. A few others asked the same thing and got the same silence in return. I couldn't tell if Slop Bucket was more injured or embarrassed. Some teachers ran up and yelled at us to get out of there. An ambulance came and took Slop Bucket away. We didn't see him again for a couple of days.

Terry sat next to me on the bus that afternoon. "We oughta do some'n 'bout Bobby," he said.

"We can't do nothin'. He can whoop all of us."

"One-on-one, sure, but not all of us at the same time."

"Everyone'll chicken out."

"Yeah," he agreed, "but you and me can take him."

I don't remember being scared. I don't ever remember being scared when I had to match wit against brawn, not until decades later when I was facing down the entire publishing industry. I was excited about the scheme Terry and I had cooked up.

We waited a week. Bobby almost always took a crap between lunch and study hall. We gave him enough time to settle into a stall and then slipped into the bathroom. I waited by the door while Terry walked up to the stall and tapped on the door.

"Hey Bobby," he whispered, "you in here?"

"Whaddya want?" Bobby growled.

"I just found out that Jerrah asked Beckah out and said he don't care if you find out 'cause he'll whoop you if you try to do anything about it."

"Nuh uh."

"Okay, you ain't gotta believe me. But they're back behind the gym right now."

"What?"

"Yeah, I'm tryin' a tell you. You better get out there."

While Bobby fumbled with his pants, I slipped out of the bathroom and ran to the spot behind the gym where students liked to fight and make out. Terry and I had already set everything up. The gym had a long row of doors that opened to the back of the school grounds. I sat on the hillside leading up to the track and waited. Along came Bobby, with Terry a few steps behind. I could practically see the steam coming out of Bobby's ears.

Terry grinned when Bobby pulled a gun on me. I tried to act properly scared. Part of the fear was real because I didn't want him to start using his fists. I talked to Bobby, trying to calm him down, but not too much, while Terry chimed in from behind. I was starting to get nervous when the gym doors burst open and the eighth-grade Phys Ed teacher, Mr. Eaves, shouted at Bobby to put down the gun. I could see Slop Bucket watching the action from a crack in the furthermost door.

"It ain't mine," Bobby said, dropping the gun and putting his hands in the air. He was paler than birchbark. Mr. Eaves ran forward and grabbed the gun.

"Let's go, Bobby."

"It ain't mine," Bobby repeated.

Mr. Eaves looked at me. "You okay?"

I was giddy. "I'm real scared," I said, hugging myself.

"Wait here. I'll send someone after you." He looked at Bobby and pulled at his elbow. "Come on."

"I told you, it ain't mine. Terrah gave it to me."

Mr. Eaves looked at Terry, who put on a show of disbelief. "Sir, I ain't got nothin' to do with no guns. Golly, I thought Bobby was gonna shoot me, too." He capped off his appeal by wiping his nose and eyes.

"Stay here with Jerry," Mr. Eaves said.

He marched Bobby away, ignoring his protests. After they were gone, Slop Bucket burst through the door with a huge smile on his face. "How'd you get him to take that gun?"

"Shit," Terry said, "I told him that he needed to send a real message to any boy stupid enough to try and steal Beckah."

"Y'all are crazy," Slop Bucket said. "He could've shot you."

"That thing ain't loaded."

The three of us kept it quiet and the rest of the school had no trouble believing that Bobby would threaten somebody with a gun. The principal expelled him, which was just as well. He wasn't matriculating and you couldn't have a kid in middle school who was old enough to buy his classmates alcohol.

So, yeah, like I said, Terry and I go way back and he's somebody I trust. He wasn't one of the popular kids, but he was a very popular kid. We were big into mama jokes and nobody could bust them like Terry. Everybody liked him, including the teachers who gave him bad grades.

There's something about fearless people that makes them likable even when they do bad stuff. My first year at Radford, a lot of our graduating class from high school stayed in touch. It wouldn't last long, as we all kind of drifted into our own little lives, but for a while we kept up the pretense of being long-term friends. By sophomore year, only Terry still made the drive over to Radford; sometimes Slop Bucket rode along. Terry was already doing what he called odd jobs for money. He didn't waste any time with community college.

One weekend when he was visiting, we were sitting around with my roommates (who also liked Terry), talking shit and playing Tecmo Super Bowl. I lived on the ground level of a three-story building with two units on each floor. From the living room, we could see everyone who came in and out. Our third-floor neighbor, Dre (short for Andrew, not Andre), pulled up, left his bike in the vestibule, and trotted up the stairs. Nobody paid Dre any mind, but Terry was staring out the window.

"That's a nice bike," he said.

"Yeah," a roommate said absently.

"How much you reckon it's worth?"

It was a Trek, in excellent condition. "At least a few hundred," I said. I knew what Terry was thinking, but didn't take him seriously until he smacked my knee and said "C'mon."

"Are you outta your mind?"

"Nah. It's easy. Make sure nobody's comin'."

My roommates put down their controllers and watched in shock as Terry casually wheeled the bike inside. I came in behind him and shut the door.

"We gotta hide this motherfucker," he said.

"Take it to the back."

We unscrewed the front wheel and crammed the two parts into my closet. Everyone stared at us when we returned to the living room.

"Don't worry about it," Terry said. "Just keep your mouth shut." His demeanor had gone from laid back to menacing. I knew the boys would follow directions.

Just then, a frantic Dre pounded on the door. Everyone looked around at one another. Terry answered as if nothing was the matter: "Wha's up, man?"

Dre burst inside the apartment. "Did you guys see what happened to my bike?"

Before anyone could say something stupid, Terry exclaimed, "Holy shit, that was *your* bike?"

"Yes! What the fuck happened to it?"

"Some guy walked over and rode it off. We thought he was one of your friends." The other guys murmured their agreement.

"Ae you serious?" Dre shouted.

"Yeah. He just picked it up and rode off."

"Which way? What does he look like?"

"White kid with a tie-dyed shirt. 'Bout yay tall. He went thataway." Terry said it like he'd been working on the plan for two days. Dre looked in the direction of Terry's finger. "That's right," Terry said, his voice excitable. "He went down there. If you hurry, you might be able to get'm."

Dre took off and Terry shut the door with a smile. "I give'm a fifty-fifty chance of catchin' the bastard," he said.

Late that night, I helped Terry load the Trek into the bed of his truck. He covered it with a tarp and there it stayed for the next day, barely hidden, as a furious Dre posted "missing bicycle" signs around the neighborhood.

# 5

Welp, looks like I went on another of those tangents. I told you it was bound to happen. I do apologize. Mama always said I was a wonderful boy right until the time I started talking.

I believe I was telling you about my conversation with Terry, who was going to the Graham-Beaver game.

"Anything interestin' afterward?" I said.

"The usual. Some of the boys'll be drinkin' over at Gary's, but I might sit it out."

Gary was another high school buddy who never left town. He drove a forklift at Pemco and had four kids, which never stopped him from hosting the gang. His wife, a girl from the West Virginia side, kicked him out about once a month, but he always came back. A shindig at Gary's house, with his surly wife and bratty children, didn't sound very exciting, but it wasn't like Terry to sit anything out. I figured he was into something best not discussed on the phone.

"Wha's goin' on over there?" he said.

If I was going to tell anyone about my literary aspirations, it would have been Terry–owing to the fact that he kept his mouth shut–but I never could bring myself to share. I didn't want to give anyone a reason to look down on me. That's how it is for writers: the luckiest ones are celebrated; the rest of us enjoy pity or scorn. "Eh, you know," I said. "I might grab a pint or two, but I'll prolly just chill at home."

"You ain't comin' in for the game, then?"

"Not this year."

"Shit, you hadn't been there for, what? Fifteen, sixteen years?"

"Some'n like that."

"Can't say I blame you."

With the small talk out of the way, I got down to business. "You know any guys who do stuff with computers?"

"Nope. Don't they give you a computer for your job?"

"I ain't lookin' to buy one. I wanna learn more about hackin', pullin' things out of the cloud, stuff like that. Figured you might know somebody in that scene."

"Can't help you there, buddy."

It wasn't an auspicious start. I came up in the last generation of people who didn't use the internet until adulthood. Some of us learned the ins-and-outs of technology, but I wasn't among them. I knew how to check email and use a Word document and that was about it. I didn't have connections among computer geeks. Missy was useless with technology, too, along with the rest of my colleagues. Asking a student sounded like trouble and I didn't know the first thing about hiring somebody, and anyway was a bit light in the wallet for that sort of move.

It seemed like the only way to get answers was to go directly to the source. So I turned my attention to finding Rodrigo.

# 6

I started with the easy stuff: email, home address, phone number, et cetera. For such a public guy, Rodrigo's basics were surprisingly hard to find. I guess he'd gotten famous enough to earn some privacy.

I went back to the internet to see if I missed anything. It was more of what I had already found: Rodrigo bitching on Twitter about white Latinxs; Rodrigo leading a BIPOC-only workshop; Rodrigo confessing to yet another mental disorder. I combed through biographical information again. He was from some Inca village with a bunch of X's in its name. I didn't recognize the name, maybe because I couldn't pronounce it. He crossed the border illegally with his mother when he was a baby. He grew up destitute in the Bronx. He got a green card through the DREAM Act. He didn't believe in the American dream, though. Rodrigo wanted to decolonize the continent.

I didn't believe a goddamn word of it.

Still, his profile raised some difficult questions for me. If Rodrigo could get so much credibility with the novel I wrote, then what did it say about my own imagination? What did it say about his audience? I don't fancy myself a literary theorist, but if there was anything good about the situation, it's that I proved I could be a successful writer. In a roundabout way, at least. Could I have succeeded in my own body? I don't like to linger on that question.

Whatever the case, I sure as shit wasn't going to let Rodrigo succeed in mine. He could hustle the gullible, he could speak the dialect of social justice, he could perform for Twitter and Instagram, but he was nothing but a content pimp without the work he took from me. That's what I kept reminding myself: in the end, writing isn't about the hullaballoo, but the pursuit of quality art. It sure seems like hullaballoo pays the bills, though.

Another thing that caught my eye was all the praise for Rodrigo's ability to write a good setting. Critics raved about Rodrigo's authentic portrayal of Appalachia, a stunning achievement for somebody from the rough-and-tumble streets of New York City. How in the world did he do it, they wondered? They expected him to do well with the Guatemalan characters, but his treatment of the white working class and rural life in America was pitch-perfect.

The migrant family at the center of *Coyote Road* ends up in Galax, Virginia, working in a furniture factory. Galax is only an hour from Radford, near North Carolina, and I took a lot of trips down while I was writing the book. It used to be a typical country town, but now it's filled with Mexican and Central American laborers. There are Latin markets and strip-mall taquerias so dingy that they'd give edgy college kids a boner. The main family in the novel is K'iche'–not Latino, per se–and so there's a lot of tension with both white and whiter people. They can feel at home in the Latin community, but there's no real Indigenous scene to participate in. I saw that tension a lot when I was in Central America: the Indian villages were a different world than Spanish Guatemala. I wouldn't say that the K'iche' hated mestizos and Spaniards or anything like that, but they sure as hell didn't trust them. A lot of those villages dealt with massacres in the recent past. They didn't really see themselves as sharing the same nation as people in the cities. I could understand where they were coming from: people in Bluefield don't share much but a passport with people in Hawaii.

I suppose that nobody complained about the novel's portrayal of Guatemala because they thought Rodrigo wrote it. Had it been published under my name, the reaction might have been different. But Rodrigo also got props for portraying Appalachia accurately, and that was entirely because of me. I didn't know why he got to rep my region without anyone asking questions, but Radford will have to give me tenure before I think too much about that kind of stuff.

The point, anyway, is that my novel had succeeded without me, which only made me more furious. I felt doubly useless. Before I discovered Rodrigo's theft, I was merely a failed author. Now I was also a failed entrepreneur.

# 7

I listened to Rodrigo on a podcast. It went like this:

**Host:** Our next guest is Rodrigo Suarez, author, activist, and multimedia artist. Suarez is a queer K'iche' who illegally crossed the border when he was a young child with his mother. He grew up in very difficult circumstances, but rose above to become the wonderful creator and visionary we see today. Welcome to the show.

**RS:** Sure.

**Host:** Let's jump right into your novel, your debut novel. It's called *Coyote Road* and it's just, wow, a stunning read. I couldn't put it down. It's about a family of K'iche'—did I pronounce that right? Okay, awesome—K'iche' migrants who end up in rural Virginia, where they have to acclimate to life as undocumented workers in a strange and hostile world. Tell us a little about your process. How did the idea come to you? How did you go about telling this amazing story?

**RS:** I mean, it wasn't an idea that came to me. It's real life. And describing it as "amazing" kind of takes away from the gravity of the novel's themes. Like, it's real, know what I mean? This is stuff that happens every single day. And it's not amazing at all to the people it happens to. So it's pretty much gaslighting to treat it is as made up or whatever. It comes from stuff I lived, that my mother lived, my abuela, you know, just generations of people who have suffered white supremacy and genocide and colonization.

**Host:** I'm so sorry, I didn't mean to suggest that the story isn't grounded in reality. Of course it is. I'm mortified by everything you've gone through, everything you continue to go through. I can't even imagine how difficult it's been. So, yeah, it's an . . . um . . . a tragedy. I guess what I meant, which I wish I would have articulated more clearly, is that you harnessed this reality in a really powerful way, right? You, um, captured something, like, hidden or incomprehensible to most people.

**RS:** Not to most people. To most white supremacists.

**Host:** Okay, but most of the book-buying public are well-off white people, correct?

**RS:** Whatever. That's not who I write for. If they learn something from my novel, that's fine, but I need them to do something more than feel bad. I need them to interrogate their privilege, to hold space for BIPOCs, you know what I'm saying? More than anything I want my BIPOC readers to feel seen, to feel heard, and I don't really care if white readers like it or not. If they like it, then they need to do something. I'm not writing for them to feel good about themselves.

**Host:** So there's an activist component to your writing?

**RS:** I don't separate art from activism. I couldn't even if I wanted to. Separating the two is pretty much the height of white privilege. I don't have the privilege of writing for entertainment. For me, it's survival. For Black writers, it's survival. For trans and nonbinary writers, it's survival. If you can write a book without thinking about its role in making a better world, then you gave up your right to say anything. Writing and reading for pleasure is some white bullshit. That's a luxury my people don't have.

**Host:** That's an interesting point of view. What I hear you saying is that–

**RS:** What I'm saying is that shit is real for us. We're not interested in beach reading. We don't have any beach to relax on. We're in survival mode, whether we're washing dishes for pennies or writing novels. Our work is our life, literally.

**Host:** So you don't believe in separating the artist from the art?

**RS:** [Chortles.] Nah, hermano, that's some fuckery that white people came up with. How do you separate them? The work is the body. The words are the soul. When you remove the artist from the art, you've killed the art, not the artist.

**Host:** Yeah that's really interesting because when I was in grad school–it feels like a hundred years ago–there was a lot of debate about the role of the artist in the creation of art. When I got my PhD, the theory craze was on its last legs, but it was still going strong. You could still apply to jobs in theory, for example. After so many years of poststructuralism, the idea of the author–

**RS:** Let me stop you here. That theory shit–that Derridean shit or whatever it's called–never applied to us. For me, for us, theory is lived experience. We have to solve the world in order to survive the world. We're not spectators, disembodied and whatnot.

**Host:** No, no, I was about to say the same thing, basically, that killing the idea of the author strikes me as incompatible with, maybe even anathema to, the subjectivity of authorship.

**RS:** But that's not what I said.

**Host:** It's not?

**RS:** No. I said that if you remove the author then you're left with the default. And what's the default? Whiteness. White supremacy, more specifically. It's a form of genocide. Indigenous peoples create art because it claims our space in this world.

**Host:** But . . . . Anyway, have you been back to Guatemala since you left as a child?

**RS:** This is really an emotional topic for me.

**Host:** We don't have to discuss it.

**RS:** It has to be discussed, no matter how difficult. That's our burden. You wouldn't understand, but it's constant so unfortunately we grow accustomed to it. And it's exhausting, right? If we don't struggle to make ourselves visible, though, then we'll disappear, which is exactly what settler society wants to happen.

**Host:** Right. So, yeah, have you been back?

**RS:** Of course not. We didn't have the money, first of all. My mother worked nonstop for little pay, and sometimes for no pay at all. If you're undocumented, the employer can treat you like dirt. He doesn't have to pay you. What are you gonna do about it? Call the cops? White supremacy structures society so that the state is never on the side of BIPOC. We had no recourse against the abuse we experienced. We're constantly erased and gaslighted, too.

**Host:** We're running out of time, but I wanted to give you a chance to discuss *Coyote Road* in your own words. What would you like to tell our audience about the novel?

**RS:** It was a labor of love, but also an expression of deep personal pain. I want them to buy it, but I don't want them to be apathetic after they read it. Do better. Be better. Black lives matter. Indigenous lives matter. Indigenous sovereignty matters. BIPOC liberation matters. Trans lives matter. The natural world matters. That's what I most want the audience to know. But they can check out my other work on my Patreon, which is linked on my Twitter and Instagram accounts.

**Host:** What are you working on right now?

**RS:** All kinds of stuff. Like I said, check out my Patreon for excerpts and updates.

**Host:** Thanks so much for joining us today.

**RS:** Yeah.

After Rodrigo had signed off, the host spent ten minutes apologizing for his insensitivity.

# 8

I thought a lot about the interview after I heard it. One thing stood out above everything else: Rodrigo's bit about white supremacy. Now, I feel like I need to make something clear, being from Bluefield and all. I don't deny that white supremacy exists, even though something feels off about the way that educated dorks talk about it on social media. Hell, not a day passed in Bluefield without me hearing some of that white supremacy Rodrigo was always on about. A lot of my friends pretend it's a myth, but they're either lying or have a really strict definition of "racism." They damn well know what they grew up saying and hearing and what still flies out of their mouths whenever diversity or immigration comes up. Not to mention that back then they had just finished voting for Trump and boasting about it to anyone who would listen. I suppose I'm trying to say that, sure, white supremacy is a thing but it also has a strange way of sounding like a whole lot of nothing.

So I didn't give much of a damn that Rodrigo was hammering on colonization and racism or whatever. If that suited him, then he could talk about it until his suspiciously thin lips fell off. The problem was that he badly misrepresented the theme of the novel—*and he was supposed to be the author.* He saw white supremacy. Fine. I don't see how you could write about migrants to the United States without exploring prejudice and what have you. He was stretching it, no doubt, but at least he wasn't inventing the theme out of thin air.

But that dipshit never mentioned trade and free markets and stuff. It was all race this, gender that. I'd spent a lot of time thinking about the connection between economic policies in Central America and Central American migration to the United States. There was a dirty war in the villages I wrote about and the aftereffects could be found in the factories of Galax, Virginia. I practically included a diagram of these connections in the novel. Rodrigo talked around the obvious problem, but he never named it directly, which I found especially dubious. I couldn't help but think that Rodrigo was enjoying his own little version of white supremacy.

The novel was mine, but I wanted to know who had written his media script. He sure as hell didn't lift it from me. I don't know, maybe it was some open-source grift because Rodrigo sounded like every other self-righteous nitwit on the internet. If somebody had trademarked certain buzzwords—gaslighting, hold space, privilege, slay, I just can't, do better—then that motherfucker would be collecting more royalties than the Beatles. The kids call it "virtue signaling," but that doesn't sound right to me. It's more like a latter-day shakedown. They're always selling something alongside the indignation.

# 9

I had found out more about Rodrigo than I ever wanted to know and it was time to do something about his theft. I reckon I spent so many hours doing research because on some level I dreaded going after him. I was mad, but I knew that Rodrigo had a serious advantage: fame. With that advantage came a gullible and needy reading public who would defend Rodrigo no matter how bad his behavior. I'd be mocked and condemned and disregarded. And God help me if anyone decided to dig around for old acquaintances in Bluefield.

I knew damn well what I was up against. People like Missy tumble their way through life with blithe optimism, and sometimes it works for them, but there's a simple formula: if you have enough money or fame, then you win. Facts don't matter. There's no shortage of ass-kissers lining up to defend their favorite celebrities and those celebrities rally together as a matter of principle.

Circumstances, not virtues, are the deciding factor in any conflict. In those times when Missy came out ahead in a brouhaha, she marked it down to good manners, but they didn't have much to do with it, really, at least not in the way she thought. Her good manners didn't win the day because virtue is persuasive; they limited her antagonist's ability to play dirty. Missy could play dirtier than anyone without even knowing it. I had no doubt that Rodrigo would play dirty, but without the good manners.

When I was a kid, one of the biggest drug dealers in town was a deputy in the Tazewell County Sheriff's Department. His name was Pearce and he came from one of the region's oldest families—the ones from Europe, anyway. He owned a mechanic shop that did most of the state vehicle inspections in town, a family pharmacy with an old-fashioned soda counter, and hundreds of acres scattered across the county. Pearce was a friendly guy, a natural gladhander, and for the decent households of Bluefield a wonderful community leader. The town's indecent people knew a different Pearce, however.

Bluefield was a hard place to deal in, not because of limited supply or clientele, but because product was confiscated at a tremendous rate. That would normally be something for a police department to boast about, but in Bluefield it was Pearce doing the confiscating, which meant that the drugs were getting back on the streets more efficiently.

I found out the hard way during senior year of high school that rumors about Pearce were true—the rumors weren't crazy enough, actually. We weren't exactly budding Scarfaces, but me and some buddies supplemented our minimum wage jobs with a side hustle here and there. Weed, mostly. We didn't have the chops or connections for cocaine and back then pills weren't really big. There were a lot of customers at Graham High and we sometimes sold to the kids at Beaver, across the state line.

Well, one Saturday night we were at the city park about to make some good business and Pearce rolled up. Everyone scattered, but my buddies and I were in the center of the crowd so we were left face-to-face with Pearce. He smiled at us. "Boys," he said, nodding.

"Hi Mr. Pearce," we mumbled in unison.

"That's quite a crowd y'all had here. You puttin' on some kind of show?"

"No, sir."

"Sellin' some'n, maybe? Lollipops and Cracker Jacks?"

"No, sir."

He grinned and in the glow of the streetlamps I could see both rows of teeth. They were straight and sparkly white. Pearce wasn't wanting for a dentist.

He said, "I'd hate to have to call your parents, boys."

"No need, sir."

"Don't get smart with me, you little pissant." He tilted his head and looked at me. "You're that Turley boy, ain'tcha? I heard plenty about you. Seems like you need to learn some manners. Your no-good daddy didn't have any, that's for sure."

"He wasn't around to teach me, anyway."

At that, Pearce unholstered his gun. He pointed it at my face and said, "Feel like servin' up any more sass, boy?"

"No, sir," I grumbled, dropping my head.

"Well, boys, it seems that we got ourselves a situation. Y'all are out here pushin' dope and that's a big problem. You're rottin' the brains of our youth. Judges don't look kindly on that." We shifted our feet and looked at the ground. He continued, "C'mon, let's see it. Show me what you're holdin'."

"We ain't got shit," I said.

"Come again?"

"We ain't got shit."

He chuckled and raised the gun. "I ain't askin' again. Show me what you're holdin'."

One of my buddies made to pull our stash out of the car, but I piped up before he got very far. "Go fuck yourself."

Pearce snorted and then whipped me across the side of my face with the barrel of the gun. I went down and my buddies backed up with their hands in the air.

"Get up," Pearce said.

This time I listened. He whipped me on the forehead as soon as I stood and back to the pavement I went. I could feel streams of blood rushing down my jawline. As I sat on the ground, gasping, Pearce struck me on the top of my skull. That pretty much put me out. Everything became fuzzy and distant. I sensed that my buddies were handing the stash to Pearce, but it could have been a head trip. They woke me up by pouring beer onto my face and slapping my cheeks. They dragged me into the car and sped away. At least we ain't in jail, they all agreed. I wasn't so reasonable. I'd rather have gotten hauled in than robbed.

I was angry for the next week and tried to think of a way to get revenge. Nothing seemed possible. I mean, what the fuck were we supposed to do about it? Go to the cops?

Everyone in school wanted to know why my face looked like a cluster of grapes. I wouldn't say and the rumors flew about who had whooped me. Nobody came forth and claimed credit, so my classmates probably figured that one of mama's lovers had given me a beating. I didn't have to make up a story for mama, though, because she never bothered to ask what had happened.

I suppose my point in telling the story is that I knew from the jump I had little recourse against Rodrigo. I'd tangled with people above my weight class a bunch of times before. Rodrigo wasn't like Pearce, but he was formidable just the same. Publishers, agents, podcasters, professors, and booksellers were invested in him—figuratively and literally. He had an exotic product to sell and a large base of consumers. He was a darling of the online activist set, a group quite adept at their own little forms of brutality. And even though I pegged him as a birdbrain, he had enough savvy to feed gullible fans the hogwash they so desperately wanted.

# 10

My first thought was to contact his publisher, but I decided against it. I didn't want to give them time to organize a response ahead of any public accusations. I would go directly to Rodrigo. He taught creative writing courses at Columbia, so I emailed his university account.

My message was polite. If there's one thing boys from Bluefield are good at, dumb or smart, it's minding our manners when needed. I didn't accuse him of plagiarism or anything like that. I told him that I'm a writer who had some thoughts about the novel and he might like to hear them. I considered it downright rude that Rodrigo didn't respond. He probably thought I was a nutjob or con artist or just a regular person fit to ignore. Bagging girls is the main reason guys want to be famous, but having social license to be an asshole is a nice little bonus.

I re-sent the message a few times with the same result. I can't say I expected him to write back, but getting ignored rubbed me the wrong way. I suspect he knew what I was getting at. I'd have to be more forthright next time.

So I sent him a different message, this one suggesting how ironic it was that he published the exact same novel I'd already written. I figured that might get his attention. He could go to his publisher and do damage control, but I'd come to realize that the battle was going public sooner or later. Without a public component, there was no plagiarism, just a sad-sack whose lunch money was taken by the teacher's pet. I was nothing. I needed Rodrigo to acknowledge me. Without that acknowledgment, I couldn't call myself a writer. You steal a man's work, you also steal his destiny.

I got no response to the second message. No surprise. Rodrigo was either not getting my emails or deleting them. I liked to think that somewhere in the mush occupying his skull, those messages gave him a flash of remorse or fear—because he knew that I was telling the truth, knew that he had done exactly what I accused him of—and that the outlandishness of my accusation made it all the more disturbing. I doubted it, though. I took Rodrigo for the kind of guy who introspects only to the degree that he can become more delusional.

I started sending messages to his agent without much hope that he actually read them. Some minion who got paid mostly in prestige probably had to sift through the agent's email account to thin out the clutter. My messages wouldn't be considered anything else. They weren't hostile enough to get a rise out of these know-it-alls and too unimportant for a response. The agent's assistant had been well-trained.

I was feeling downright melancholy in those days. It's not fun being ignored, even if you detest the people ignoring you—hell, *especially* if you detest them. Hatred ain't worth a shit without some cooperation. What really had me down was a feeling of powerlessness. There I was, sitting on the most obvious case of plagiarism in the history of written language, and I wasn't sure what to do about it. I wasn't sure anything could be done.

When people are feeling powerless, they often see violence as their only option. An enemy's got the entire force of a country or society on his side, then what else is left to do but sock him in the goddamn chin? There's a certain dignity to applying an old-fashioned beatdown. I didn't have access to Rodrigo, but I was feeling punchy in the same way. I turned up the temperature on my emails, addressing them to Rodrigo and cc'ing the agent.

After about half a dozen tries, I finally heard back. It was the agent, who had taken Rodrigo out of the address line:

> Mr. Turley:
>
> I have reviewed your claims about *Coyote Road* and find them absolutely without merit. I kindly request that you no longer contact myself or Mr. Suarez. If you persist in this harassment, I will have no choice but to notify the proper authorities.
>
> Sincerely Yours,
> Craig Toney
> Principal, Toney Literary Group

I chortled at "proper authorities." No matter how radical these eggheads wanted to be, calling the cops was always their first impulse. The proper authorities didn't worry me a single bit. It was the politeness of the message that frightened me.

# 11

Amid this period of sadness, I decided to hit the town and see if I couldn't get into something fun. Radford didn't have many options for professionals such as myself and I didn't want to go all the way to Blacksburg because I knew I'd be getting drunk. In college, I'd driven those old mountain roads under the influence dozens of times, but at my age it was a terrible idea. I no longer had the energy to gamble or get arrested.

I showered and gave myself a spritz of the Bulgari cologne I'd owned for eight or nine years. I didn't dress up, but made enough of an effort to where nobody would confuse me for a slob. I hopped in my 1995 Altima and headed to Macado's, a sandwich joint that had been around since my student days. (There was one in the mall in Bluefield and to people of my station it was the height of luxury.) My grad school cohort went there occasionally, but Macado's was mostly a faculty hangout, with a few townies thrown in. The place had a large and lively bar area with plenty of TVs. I arrived as it was getting dark and took a spot at the counter.

There was no talent around, so I sipped on a rum with coke and waited for the bar to fill up. (You might have thought that I drink bourbon, but it always tasted like diesel fumes to me.) I didn't feel like getting sucked into conversation with any of the middle-aged men at the bar, so I kept my gaze on the screens showing college football. People kept trickling in and soon the restaurant was buzzing with activity. Nobody worth hitting on had showed up and I was thinking about packing it in when I heard somebody call, "Hey, Professor Turley!"

I turned around and saw a group of first-year grad students, young and earnest and filled with possibility. I smirked at hundreds of long-ago memories. The entire cohort wasn't out at Macado's, of course. Each cohort had some older students, people with real jobs and families. But the majority were fresh out of undergrad, enjoying that fleeting period where a person is dumb enough to imagine a decent future.

The person who had called my name was Natalie and she was in her late twenties, just young enough to join her peers on the bar circuit every now and again. I used to serve as a faculty mentor to the teaching fellows, but gave it up after a couple of years. I decided I'd rather take on an extra class than bullshit a bunch of neophytes about the majesty of teaching. I was still familiar with each incoming class of grad students, though. GTFs were the pride of the department. The chair introduced each of them by name at the year's first faculty meeting and they could often be found hanging around the photocopier and teachers' lounge. Natalie wasn't like anyone in her cohort, or like anyone in the entire department, really. She had a way about her that suggested a whole lot of excitement.

"Good evenin'," I said in response to her greeting. The group stood around awkwardly until Natalie broke the tension. "We're getting a table. Do you wanna join us?" Her peers nodded and implored me to say yes. I pretended to think on it for a second before accepting. I followed Natalie to the table. She was wearing a mid-length skirt made of striped knit fabric that hugged tightly against her. As she moved among the mass of pasty-faced frat boys and middle-agers in their TJ Maxx khakis, she repelled all the energy around her. "She don't belong here," I thought to myself. "She ought to be in a TV show set in some big city." It's weird how we can be in a place but not of a place. Like we're there but somewhere else, forever in conflict with our surroundings. Anyway, at the time I sure wasn't thinking about geography. I shook my head in appreciation. This life wasn't always hard luck.

It took us a while to loosen up, but once we got started it was a merry time. The students thought it was cool to drink with faculty, even though they probably knew that I wasn't a real professor. The topic of universal truth came up and one of the students asked if I believe in it.

"Sure do," I said.

This answer riled them up–they all thought the notion was absurd–and started in on their rejoinders.

"How can you make any judgment beyond your own Eurocentric standards?" Natalie wanted to know.

"What's that got to do with universal truth?" I said.

"Like, everything?"

"You can't say that unless you believe in universal truth, at least implicitly."

"That doesn't make any sense."

"But it does," I said, smiling at the table. "You're hung up on what I'm gettin' wrong, but ain't no wrong in a world governed by relativity."

"I'm just saying that our perspectives are limited by experience, so you can't know the world from a Black person's point of view or a woman's point of view."

"I agree."

"So you *don't* believe in universal truth."

Actually, I didn't give a single fuck about truth, universal or otherwise. It was the sort of topic that fascinated new grad students at middling universities. My cohort had quibbled about the same thing. Back then, just like now, I took whatever position might make the conversation less boring. My truths were simple: I was a bit smitten with Natalie, I was an unpublished writer, and Rodrigo Suarez stole my novel. These truths didn't have to belong to anyone else.

"Now I didn't say that," I laughed. "Your side of the issue has an unfair advantage."

Natalie laughed in return. "What? No it doesn't."

"Sure it does. All you gotta say is that a Mexican can't understand a Korean and you're done. But the way I see it, all our experiences being different is the ultimate universal truth."

"No, that's a truism, not a truth."

"Okay, I'll try another one."

"Go for it." She raised her eyebrows ever so slightly, sending shivers throughout my midsection. It was an innocent gesture on the surface, but lurid in its execution.

"I was born in Bluefield, West Virginia. Now go ahead and tell me how that ain't the truth."

"Factoid. Not a truth."

"So what we're really arguin' is definitions?"

"That's the only thing anyone argues over when you think about it."

It seemed that the rest of the table, and the restaurant surrounding it, had faded into the night and Natalie and I were alone, stuck in one another's company. It went on that way for a few hours. Others occasionally intruded on our conversation, but we quickly closed ourselves off to their presence. Our knees touched often enough to suggest that our night wouldn't end at Macado's. Before we knew it, everyone started paying their tabs.

"Go on without me," Natalie told her ride. "Professor Turley is giving me some career advice."

Her friends looked amused. They knew damn well what I was giving Natalie. Their smiles suggested that they approved. The old lady of the group decided to have a little fun. After they cleared out, I asked for our tabs and paid them both.

Natalie touched my arm and whispered, "Let's continue our conversation in a more private place?"

"It's no palace, but my house is clean and quiet."

I tried not to leer at her on the drive home, but she made it difficult. She kept doing this coquettish thing where she bunched her shoulders and pressed her legs together, all the while letting her tongue slide across her upper lip. Once inside, we didn't do much conversing. I shut the door and we practically collided into each other. I led her to the back of the house and explored beneath her skirt until both of us were ready to explode. My earlier reading of Natalie turned out to be correct: she brought an energy to the bedroom that had me praying and exalting more than a country preacher. After we finished, Natalie went into the bathroom to clean up. I was splayed out on the bed, too satisfied and tired to move.

She came out of the bathroom, still naked, and stood at the foot of the bed, an uncertain look on her face. "Well, um, I guess I'd better go."

"You can stay if you like."

She smiled and lay next to me on the bed. I lit a joint and offered it to her. We passed it back and forth, watching the smoke expand throughout the ill-lit bedroom smelling of body fluid and marijuana ash.

"I'm gonna read for a bit," she said and went to the living room to retrieve her shoulder bag. She settled back into bed with a book and clicked on the table lamp. I'm the kind of guy who likes to know what book everyone's holding, so I leaned forward and glanced over. I fell back onto my pillow with a grunt.

She was reading *Coyote Road.*

My heart started pumping extra oxygen to my extremities, which I suppose is why I suddenly got sloppy. They say that after a man spends himself, he can think most clearly. It sure as hell wasn't true in this case because I couldn't control myself despite a warning bell in the back of my brain.

"Whatcha readin'?" I said.

She rested the book on her lap and smiled. "It's called *Coyote Road.*"

"Any good?"

"Oh my God it's *soooo* good. We're reading it for our Indigenous literature seminar."

"Hmmm."

"I'm surprised you haven't read it yet."

"Well, here's the thing," I said, rolling onto my side to face her. "I have an issue with that book."

"What?"

"It's kinda hard to explain."

She tussled my hair and gave me the lurid smile that had churned up my insides all night long. "Try."

To this day, I don't know what the hell I was thinking. I reckon I was feeling mighty comfortable with Natalie and wanted to release some of the stress I'd been carrying. Whatever the reason, I knew it was a huge mistake the moment I finished saying, "I wrote that book."

Natalie's smile went away and she pulled back her hand. "What do you mean?"

"I wrote *Coyote Road.* That motherfucker stole it from me. It's plagiarized." I was committed by that point.

"But, like . . . I don't understand."

"It ain't complicated. I wrote the book. Rodrigo stole it from me."

"Stole it how?" Her tone was that of a nurse speaking to a mental patient.

"I don't know. I'm tryin'a figure it out. But he damn sure stole it. No doubt about it."

"Do you know him?"

"Never met'm in my life."

"Did you email him a copy?"

"Nope."

"So how could he have stolen anything from you?"

"A slush pile, the cloud, I don't fuckin' know." The frustration was directed at her but squarely aimed at myself.

"You know what," she said, hopping off the bed and trying to cover her crotch and chest with her arms, "it's almost light outside and I have to prepare for class. So I'd better be going. I'll see you around, Jerry, um, I mean, Professor Turley."

I didn't try to stop her. I'd never seen anyone get dressed so fast.

"You know what, Professor Turley? You can't know whether truth is universal or not if you don't even know what truth means."

She scampered off before I could respond.

# 12

As you might imagine, I was now extremely motivated to get justice. I worried about Natalie telling everyone my secret, but calmed down after a bit. She probably didn't want anything to do with what I told her. Sometimes a story is so crazy that people will look at you funny just for passing it along.

The day after my tryst with Natalie, I decided that I had dicked around long enough. I set up a Twitter account, @TheRealRodrigo, with *Coyote Road* as the profile picture. I had no choice but to try my hand at the damnable platform that men of my generation like to blame for all of society's ills. Twitter seemed straightforward at first but it still confused the dickens out of me. I didn't need to make a career of the platform, though, so I told myself to just type my point and send it. I kept it clear and simple: "Rodrigo Suarez did not write *Coyote*

*Road.* The entire novel is plagiarized. I am the actual author and have the evidence to prove it."

I wasn't sure what to expect, which was probably good because nothing happened. Without any followers, there was nobody to read the message, so I retweeted it myself. Still nothing. I was screwing around elsewhere on the internet when someone finally responded. I clicked on the notification: "tf is this?????"

I had to look up "tf" and discovered that people were now too lazy to write out one-syllable words or else they were scared to cuss out loud. I typed a careful answer to the reply: "This is the fucking truth. Rodrigo Suarez stole my novel. I wrote *Coyote Road.*"

"u ok dude?"

"Sure am. Are you?"

I got no further response. That was enough of Twitter for the evening. I tried again in the morning with a similar message. I still had no followers and not even the illiterate jackass bothered to reply. I wasn't deterred. I continued sending out variations of the same accusation. The entire Twitter-sphere continued ignoring me. I realized that I should be tagging certain accounts: Rodrigo, the agent, the publisher, a few media outlets. This tactic still didn't get a response. I kept at it, anyway. I didn't have anything better to do. I'd already spent my creative energy on a book that was no longer mine.

One afternoon I checked my account—logging on had become second nature and I didn't think I'd ever be able to kick the habit—and actually had a bunch of notifications. I could feel the dopamine rushing into my chest. The publisher had quote-tweeted one of my missives: "This allegation is completely without merit. We consider it defamatory of Rodrigo Suarez and if it continues we intend to seek appropriate recourse."

Appropriate recourse? My belly flab began to jiggle. Not much is funnier than an uptight goober trying to talk tough. There were lots of replies to sort through, but I paused to consider why the publisher would bring attention to accusations from a zero-follower account that nobody was paying attention to.

Did they want to shut me down? There was no need. I was yelling into a void.

Did they just get off on intimidating people with less power? Always a possibility, but it sure seemed like a waste of time in this case.

Did they want controversy to drum up sales? Why, though? The novel was a bestseller already.

Turns out that somebody had retweeted me, so my accusation circulated a bit before the publisher spoke up. Some other author with a smaller following than Rodrigo, but also with a blue checkmark (those things were important back in the day). I assumed that they had some kind of beef. People in the literary world detest each other, especially the ones who are friends. Retweeting allows them to deploy a proxy for their pettiness. I didn't care why. This lesser author had put me in business.

A smattering of people started following my account. Rodrigo's detractors, no doubt. And maybe some admirers, too. They love the tabloid thrill of online drama. Real middle-school shit, but they like to pretend it's high culture.

I smiled, picturing a furious Rodrigo frantically emailing his handlers, becoming more flustered and defensive by the second, demanding that they do something about this anonymous ingrate. Rodrigo was the kind of guy who took any opportunity to complain about being mistreated. He probably considered anything other than ass-kissing to be mistreatment.

I lit up and started reading the comments. Most were indignant on Rodrigo's behalf: why would anyone believe this anonymous account, created less than a month ago, making wild claims about a brilliant new literary voice? And where was this "proof" it claimed to have?

Well, I expected the skepticism so it didn't bother me much. I was more bothered by the notion that I didn't have any proof. The proof was in my hard drive. It was in my research. It was in my travel history. It was in my memory. It was in my very being. None of that was good enough for the public.

"But Jerry," you might be saying, "it's easy to show proof: just share your own file of *Coyote Road.*" I wish it had been that easy. What good would showing the file do? Rodrigo would never have to show his. He had published the latest version of my manuscript. If anything, it would look like I stole the novel from him.

I was pretty happy that my complaint got some traction. Yeah, the response wasn't favorable to me, but at least somebody had listened. That's all a person wants sometimes, the courtesy of an audience. I decided to keep pressing. I'd take the publisher's threats seriously when I got a letter from its lawyer.

I did everything I could to make a case. I explained my journeys in Central America, my painstaking research, my experience of Appalachia, my inspiration for the story, my long days in a K'iche' village.

The last point really raised people's dander. How dare I, presumably a white American, try to claim authenticity just because I took a vacation when Rodrigo was from the very place I'd visited? And not just from there. Indigenous to it. I didn't make it a point to argue with everyone who objected. Besides, a lot of the pushback was name-calling, which hardly fazed me. I heard ten times worse every single day growing up. I tried to keep to fact, but it was tempting to go all in on the fisticuffs. My better senses won out. In the end, I wasn't out to prove a point, but to win. I needed to be smart about it.

Besides, based on his comments, I knew that I was under Rodrigo's skin. He couldn't help himself. He always had to say something. And when he did, dozens of fellow blue checks lined up to lick his boots. But I could sense the anxiety underlying his bravado. Causing the guy some distress was a good enough start, the way I saw it.

# 13

The social media shenanigans went on for a while and hardly anything changed. Rodrigo called me "cabron mentiroso" and "un gran pendejo." I thought about replying with "como tu mama," but restrained myself in light of the bigger picture. I didn't want to blow my wad on cheap rejoinders. I'd wait for a better opportunity to come along.

Then Missy sent a message to the English Department listserv:

> Howdy everyone! I hope y'all are keeping in good spirits during this spell of cold weather. I'm writing because I just learned that Rodrigo Suarez, author of the bestselling novel Coyote Road, will be giving a reading at Virginia Tech in the spring semester! It's such exciting news! Suarez is one of the best young novelists in the country and Coyote Road is a must-read. I know that some of us teach it already. I'm hoping we can put together an

> effort to have Suarez give a reading at Radford and perhaps do some workshops with our students. Stay tuned! More to come!

I let my foul mood abate before phoning up Missy. Usually I'd visit her in person, but I was getting too old to trudge around in freezing weather.

"Professor Missy!" she answered in singsong.

"Hey, it's me."

"Well, Jerrah, I thought I'd never hear from you again."

"Sorry 'bout that. Things have been a bit hectic." I could tell already that Natalie hadn't snitched me out. She would have been a keeper, Natalie. I fucked that one up real good.

"Wha's goin' on?"

"Eh, not too much."

"I thought you just said things are hectic?"

I never did give Missy enough credit for her brains. "Anyway, I just got your email."

"Which one?"

"About that Suarez fella."

"Oh, yeah. Ain't it excitin'?"

"Well, that's just the thing. I'm not exactly sure what he would bring to Radford, to be honest. This place is a bit conservative for that guy, ain't it?"

"No, not at all. Why would you say that? I'm teachin' *Coyote Road* in my Intro to Appalachian Studies class and the students just love it."

"Appalachian Studies?"

"Don't be so narrow-minded, Jerrah. A lot of it takes place in Galax. Appalachian don't mean white."

"Fine, fine. I'm just not sure about this guy, that's all."

"Why?" It was more a rebuke than a question.

"He's been accused of plagiarism. Did you know that?"

"I heard some'n about some nutjob harassin'm on Twitter. You can't possibly take it seriously?"

"Why not? So what if the guy makin' the accusations is a nobody. Suarez wouldn't steal from somebody famous, would he?"

"Jerrah, I really don't understand you sometimes."

That was my cue to pull back. I was in no condition to deal with Missy's disappointment. She could manage guilt like a circus juggler.

"I don't know," I said, "I reckon I'm in a mood today."

"Wha's the matter? Wha's wrong?"

"You wouldn't believe me if I told you."

"C'mon, now."

"Shit, it's nothin' worth worryin' about, anyway."

"If you say so."

"You know, more and more it feels like I'm in some simulation, like everything I've ever done somehow belongs to another person, like, another person who don't even seem real. I don't know, like I can't tell the difference between reality and my imagination."

"Oh, Jerrah, you can be so silly sometimes."

"Ain't that the truth."

# 14

I tried to think of a time that I went to war with somebody and didn't come out on top. Pearce, I guess, but that was hardly a fair fight. I'm not trying to boast, but I had a damn good track record. I don't know why, precisely. I was always good at figuring out the nuts and bolts of a situation and then knowing when to build and when to dismantle. With Rodrigo, though, I was running out of ideas. He wasn't some intimidating adversary—I refused to give him any more credit than he needed—but the situation was unfavorable to me. I wasn't just taking on Rodrigo. I had to deal with all the toadies attached to Rodrigo, as well.

Only one conflict from the past stands out as difficult and I was a kid when it happened. Coach Robbie Meadows, from a prominent family in Bluefield; a couple of his ancestors had been good at football. I remember it was my last year of little league, sixth grade, because I never played organized baseball again.

We used to practice on a nice field near the highway ramp and Coach Meadows filled the grounds with his booming voice. He'd run around the outfield, showing us where to line up and how to track fly balls. His son was the star of the team–men like Robbie Meadows didn't bother to coach children's sports unless their sons were better than everyone else. Coach didn't show much favoritism, though. He took an interest in all of us, as both a little league coach and the sixth-grade Phys Ed teacher.

He took a particular interest in me. I never liked the way he grabbed and massaged my shoulders and something felt off about the way he slapped my butt. All the coaches in Bluefield were butt-slappers, but Coach Meadows did it at the weirdest times, like when I was pacing the dugout or on my way to mama's car.

Then he started keeping me in the locker room after gym class. He'd stand next to me and prop up his foot on the bench, the bulge in his shorts directly in my line of vision. Sometimes he leaned in so closely that I could smell the stale chaw on his breath.

Needless to say, I didn't like it a single bit. Sure, I was a kid with an inattentive mama and a no-good stepdaddy, but that didn't mean I'd just bend over for the guy. I knew what he was getting at. I was determined to keep it from happening.

I didn't know what to do about the problem, though. Like I said, Coach Meadows was a big-timer in Bluefield. The coaches could get away with damn-near anything. The community thought they were gods and the administrative offices were filled with them. I was nothing but another punk kid who needed some discipline. Coach Meadows was exactly the kind of guy I should be spending time with.

I thought and thought about it but couldn't come up with any solutions. The fear kept me from thinking straight. It was a terrible fear, deep in my stomach. I was constantly at the edge of panic, aware despite my inexperience that Coach Meadows was aiming to put me in horrible pain. Whatever images I could muster filled me with nausea. Being near him made me convulse with dread.

So I kept on thinking and decided that the only way to defeat a powerful man is to bring him off on his own stupidity. As I was sorting through various memories and episodes, my mind stopped on one of my classmates, Benji. His older brother had been caught humping his girlfriend backstage of the school auditorium. Benji's brother became a folk hero, but administrators and the PTA and local clergy became obsessed with making sure no other incident occurred on school property. The principal outlawed hand-holding and school employees were on high alert for French kissing. They didn't cancel school dances—those things brought in good money—but chaperones were stationed outside the cafeteria to make sure no couples sneaked off. It was some real *Footloose*-type shit.

The silliest sex scandal could bring down even the most upstanding citizen. Nobody stood taller than Coach Meadows. But he had an Achilles heel. Proverbially, of course. Coach Meadows' Achilles heel was located a few feet up from his ankles.

One day after practice, I went with him to his office, a cinderblock closet that reeked of jockstraps and instant coffee. I had told mama to pick me up half an hour after practice would end. When everyone else cleared out, Coach Meadows told me to follow him, as I knew he would. He had a shit-eating grin when we set off to the building.

Well, I don't know how comfortable you are with explicit content, so I'll keep it short and to the point. I managed to keep my pants on by playing dumb, which didn't require too much acting, to be honest. So he had to go first. He was a big, experienced man who needed to show me a thing or two about how the body works. He was having a good tug and invited me to take over for him when I pulled an instant camera out of my backpack, snapped a picture of his midsection, and ran until I was a good sight away from school grounds. I collapsed on the bench in front of The Little Store.

(I don't know how it was listed in the Yellow Pages, but that's what everyone called it: The Little Store. It was smack dab in the middle of a neighborhood and was about the size of a cabin. The old woman who ran it used to serve hamburgers from a tiny grill nestled behind a chip rack.)

I kept a lookout for Coach Meadows. If he got hold of me, he would deliver severe retribution and take the camera. I had to be extra quick, so I didn't know if the camera caught anything incriminating or if what it caught would be lucid. Judging by his reaction, I caught enough to cause him lots of trouble. I still don't know. I never developed the pictures. There was no way to do it without the whole town finding out. I told all the kids about it, though. And I'd have the camera if I ever needed it.

Coach Meadows should have known to look for me at The Little Store, but he never turned up. I carefully made my way over to the main road and sat at the bottom of an embankment at the edge of school property, waiting for mama to arrive.

"You musta had a nice practice with that big ol' smile on your face," she said as I jumped into the passenger seat.

"Yes'm."

"Hit a home run?"

"No, ma'am."

"Well then wipe that goofy grin off your face. You look like a damn nincompoop."

I followed mama's order but kept smiling on the inside. I knew that nobody would be bothering me anymore. It was a scary and satisfying victory and I never wanted to lose the nice feeling flittering throughout my stomach in that moment.

What happened next? Nothing, which is exactly what I was hoping for.

To this day Coach Meadows is known as Handjob Rob.

# 15

Rodrigo was more formidable than Coach Meadows. The stakes were different, although I was hard-pressed to determine which situation was more messed up. Coach Meadows wanted to do something horrible, no doubt, but Rodrigo's theft somehow felt more intimate. He had lifted a tangible object from my possession, but also something abstract and irreplaceable.

The fact that his theft was so personal made it difficult to seek recourse. How do you remedy an abstraction? And how do you take on an adversary who enjoys built-in support from a devoted audience? My own uselessness came into focus with a terrible clarity. If I were to overcome Rodrigo, I'd need social capital. Brains were damn-near pointless. Success wasn't a question of guile. It was a matter of public relations.

I suspected there was more to learn about Rodrigo, so back to the internet I went. This time I kept away from podcasts and that kind of stuff. I explored public records, employment databases, ancestry sites, and so forth.

If Rodrigo wanted to play dirty, then he wouldn't be lacking for material. You could find arrest records for me in Tazewell, Mercer, and Montgomery counties. Nothing too shocking, mind you, but Americans are pretty uptight about crime. Hell, they build entire neighborhoods and highways to get away from a bit of debauchery. And that's all I'd ever been hauled in for: some old-fashioned debauchery. Drugs and fistfights. Stuff that doesn't even register in terms of real criminal behavior, the heavy-duty shit that starts at the top.

I had to be careful not to gather info that would actually help my enemy. I didn't want to give him more credibility, like he's a real gangster or whatever, an authentic street person. I grew up around goons, low-level and high. I fought with them, I schemed with them, and I eventually ran away from them. I even shot one in the face. I know what goons look and sound like. Rodrigo didn't fit the bill. He was soft. He didn't seem like the type to have survived his own story. His entire lexicon was that of a poser.

My research would turn up nothing to change this perception. But it validated the hell out of my suspicion that Rodrigo was a poser.

You see, I ended up on a fascinating trail of public records, a few of which I had to pay for, and they led to one unmistakable conclusion: that son of a bitch was no more indigenous to the Americas than kudzu.

Rodrigo Suarez was born Jason Onoufriadis in Orland Park, Illinois, son of Nikos and Angela (nee Moore). He attended DePaul for three semesters before dropping out and changing his name. He emerged about a decade later as a bestselling author. I couldn't find much about his life during the period between his name change and literary success. He had been involved with various activist groups in New York City: the Democratic Socialists of America, the LGBTQ+ Alliance, ACT UP, various election campaigns. He did the usual online yelling and accumulated a decent amount of clout, but his turn to novel-writing was abrupt and immediately successful. Maybe his transition from online influencer to bestselling author was more natural than I wanted to allow. Whatever you might say about his writing, he was certainly good at reinvention.

I sat back with a feeling of great satisfaction. "*That lyin' motherfucker*," I said out loud, a half-smile on my face. I could almost respect the hustle, but I wouldn't allow it to go on at my expense. I had known on some level that Rodrigo was making up a background. It wasn't just his looks. I mean, his looks were definitely a tip-off, but it was something about the way he sounded, the way he carried himself. He was like Natalie in the bar: not of the place in which he existed. I'm not claiming to be an expert on the K'iche', but I'd hung around a bunch of them and not a single one was anything like Rodrigo.

The stuff I found was a gamechanger. I finally had a bit of leverage. Even Rodrigo's biggest fan couldn't overlook the fact that he was a fake Indian. Suddenly, he and I were exactly the same as far as the internet was concerned: two useless cis white males. I was pretty surprised that he got away with it for so long, but I couldn't be bothered to explore why he had.

I swallowed an Adderall and took to Twitter.

# 16

Things didn't quite go according to plan. Looking back on it, I suppose I should have thought through the possibilities more carefully. Turns out that the internet didn't consider me and Rodrigo exactly the same. Nor did the internet banish Rodrigo for playing Indian. Most people didn't seem to care.

Maybe that's not the right way to put it: most people didn't seem to care about the truth of the situation. They kept on reinventing Rodrigo as needed to win an argument. The facts I'd uncovered weren't actually factual. They were ideologies. They were narratives. And in the end they didn't matter. It was an act of violence to have dug into Rodrigo's past.

Don't get me wrong: Rodrigo had plenty of detractors, but not nearly enough to end his con job. If anything, he gained more fans than he lost. I was the bad guy merely for checking up on Rodrigo's genealogy. I was a settler, a racist, a eugenicist. I was the symptom of a sick colonial system obsessed with blood quantum.

I won't sit here and try to tell you that I'm a saint, but I wasn't *that* bad. The way I saw it, a lot of people were in line ahead of me when it came to the sins of American history. I didn't care too much that people were calling the United States a fake country; I was mostly bothered that Rodrigo was fixing to survive what I thought would be a deathblow. It turned out that my biology was much more important than his.

Arguing facts, I quickly learned, wouldn't get me anywhere. The real question was why I felt the need to investigate Rodrigo in the first place. Saying that he stole my novel wasn't a good reason. It made my sin even worse.

Some influential people were willing to look past the messenger. Yeah, my stink stuck to them, but they weren't willing to brush off the fact that some douchebag from the Midwest decided he was Native American. Nobody disputed the accuracy of my research. They simply argued about its relevance and the means by which it was acquired, with a long tangent or two about the complicated nature of identity.

No doubt I came out of it worse than Rodrigo, but I sensed that my findings had damaged him–if not his career, then at least his psyche. In any event, he had a lot more to lose; my antagonist had already expropriated all the influence and money I stood to lose. Rodrigo knew it, too. He had one conniption after another on Twitter, writing long threads that condemned everything under the sun except for his own dishonesty. It played well with most of his fans, but fakery was now part of his profile, always subject to a quick insult or a good reckoning if he ran afoul of the wrong people.

# 17

Here's the sad damn truth: I was an old fart in the online world whose subcultures had long been established without my participation when all of this stuff was going down. My new Twitter addiction taught me lots of new things, but there are certain norms and unwritten rules on social media that were downright alien to me. I didn't get the memes and acronyms. I kept an Urban Dictionary tab open at all times. Having it out with somebody online put me at a steep disadvantage because I was unfamiliar with the territory. It wasn't like a brick-and-mortar conflict. Online, we were nothing more than bitchy little pixels.

But sometimes the internet decided to infringe on real life, as when one of Rodrigo's prominent supporters tweeted, "FYI: @RealCoyoteRoad is a guy named Gerald Turley. He teaches English at Radford University in Virginia."

I knew what had happened wasn't good; I just didn't know it had a name. Getting doxed was apparently a big deal with a whole set of complicated dynamics. Sometimes it was a no-no, other times it was cool. The Twitter community was divided on whether I deserved it.

Soon enough, users started tagging Radford's account.

"Hey Radford, are you aware that you employ a racist sack of shit?"

"It's disgraceful that you let this man be around students."

"How long will Radford University allow a eugenicist to stay on its faculty?"

"You need to get rid of this fraud."

And on and on.

Somehow I had become the crook, the phony, the shit-stirrer. I didn't take kindly to it. I'm nothing if not earnest. But the internet didn't care. The internet made you into whatever its users wanted you to be. My sense of proportion and space was suddenly off-kilter. I didn't feel human any longer. It's hard to explain. It's like I could no longer distinguish reality from a string playing out on the internet, as if reality itself was just an elaborate trick to keep me alive. Terrible things were happening to me and yet nothing was happening, if that makes any sense. I wasn't surrounded by a physical mob, I wasn't having a heart attack, I wasn't getting into a gunfight. I was just some asshole on a computer. Yet I couldn't ignore the forces out of my sight that threatened to undo my entire life.

It put me in mind of an experience I had hiking a popular spot for expats not far from Guatemala City. I used to go regularly with a group of Americans and Canadians. The trail ran along a narrow river for a mile or two before breaking off into an incline that scaled a few thousand feet of elevation. At the top was a bald dome with a glorious view of various volcanoes to the south and west.

The hike was rewarding but not too difficult, which made it popular with foreigners. They could put on the appearance of an urbane, outdoorsy type without actually moving across the land like a native. The hike was mostly a leisurely thing. We'd get to the top and eat sandwiches and nuts, maybe pass around a bowl and fantasize about how cool it would be to get hold of some shrooms or peyote. Then we'd walk back down filled with self-satisfaction as if we'd done something rare and magnificent, as if we'd conquered an undiscovered country. Hiking and visiting outdoor markets made us feel like we were better than tourists. We cared enough about the place to participate in a foreign version of civic life.

One day I decided to do the hike alone as preparation for harder excursions. I wanted to explore more remote places in the countryside. The usual stuff was too safe and boring. I didn't tell anyone about my plans and hopped on a bus heading out of the city without anyone seeing me.

Everything was different by myself. The first thing I noticed was how stupid the expats looked in their hiking boots and bandanas. They all wore the same knee-length cargo shorts, navy blue or gunmetal, and vintage tees with supposedly ironic messaging. I mean, I always knew they looked stupid, but it never registered so clearly until I wasn't in the middle of them. Another thing I noticed is how many amazing sounds I missed in the jungle because the expats never stopped talking: birdsong and insect calls and a whole bunch of the unknown. It was a million times more pleasant than hearing about the great new bar or pupuseria somebody had just discovered. It was always the same with the expats: discovering authentic shit catered to northerners. They thought that redundancy was the height of sophistication.

On that day, I didn't stop at the top of the mountain. I kept going down the other side, which had seen some foot traffic over the years but was still wild and overgrown. I'd been wanting to go somewhere that required a machete and, wouldn't you know it, I had managed to do it finally, but without the machete. I walked not knowing where I was going and when it came time to leave I had little idea which direction to walk. The logical thing would have been to go back the way I came, but I hadn't traveled in a straight line. I was all over the place, depending on where the jungle allowed me to move. So I relied on my instinct, which wasn't much of a guide. Back in Tazewell County I could have figured out where to go, but I was in an entirely new place. Well, it was new to me, anyway.

And that's when it hit me: all this stuff about finding something new was the oldest scam in the book. Everyone's dying to be the first to do this, the first to do that. For good reason. It usually makes them rich and famous. I've spent my life hearing about the first guy to climb Mt. Everest or swim across the Nile or contact an unknown tribe in Papua New Guinea. But when you think about it, it's all bullshit. They weren't the first to do anything, just the first to have it recorded by Western newspapers. Somebody did all that stuff already and never got a damn bit of credit. Things had to be written in a certain way, in certain places, for certain readers.

Besides, no tribe has ever been unknown. They all knew other tribes. It's like they didn't even exist until some dork in a safari hat showed up with a monocle and a notebook. What the hell does it even mean to discover a new group of people? I discover new groups of people every time I leave the house. The whole damn arrangement suddenly began to annoy me.

To make matters worse, I was lost and miserable. Wandering around all pissed off about some half-assed epiphany made my situation even worse. I no longer had any motivation to find my way to civilization. Everything I had ever known was a fraud. And I know it sounds crazy, but there's no way I could have had the epiphany anywhere else. I needed someplace pristine to show me that I was useless, even though there was nothing pristine about the place I was lost in. That's the craziest thing about it: I was trying to sort a bunch of categories in my mind that no longer mattered. The damp, uneven forest was the perfect setting for my confusion. The only thing I could make out clearly was my complete disorientation. I wandered amid that vibrant green brush and those pearly volcanic pebbles in search of absolutely fucking nothing.

I was in this state of vertigo until a few locals found me curled beneath a netleaf oak, shivering and starved half to death.

That's how it felt with Rodrigo—like I had been cheated out of an opportunity to enjoy my own confusion. Everything felt precarious in return. Unknown forces were out there, waiting to ruin my life, but there was no guarantee that those forces existed somewhere other than my own imagination.

Although my scheme to cancel Rodrigo had backfired, things weren't all bad. Fighting on the internet was a give and take. Success or failure couldn't be determined by traditional metrics. I had landed a few jabs and put some doubt in the tiny collective brain of Rodrigo's fanbase. And I couldn't deny one obvious upside to the entire mess: after decades of anonymity, I had finally made a name for myself.

# 18

It didn't take long for all that abstract stuff to become tangible. A few days after the doxing, I got a call from Missy.

"You in your office?" Her voice lacked its usual pep.

"Yeah. Why?"

"I'll be over in five minutes."

Even though I wasn't going anywhere, it felt like I had been summoned. Missy had that stern, schoolmarmish tone she liked to use when somebody had disappointed her. Sure enough, she was knocking on my door five minutes later. I gestured for her to sit down, but she ignored me and stood close to the door with a fist stuck to the side of her abdomen. I realized how much Missy had aged since we first met. Her hips were round and powerful and her hair was blown straight into a bobbed amber helmet. She reminded me of a flight attendant working the first-class cabin. She sighed before speaking.

"Jerrah Turley, what in the world is goin' on?" She sounded every bit the country matriarch she had long dreamed of becoming.

"Not much."

"Not much? Why are you harassin' that poor boy?"

"Now, Missy, you know I'd never do such a thing."

She closed her eyes and shook her head. The fist dug deeper into her side. "What've I been seein' on the internet, then?"

"Oh, you have a Twitter account? What's your handle? I'll follow you."

"Stop that sass, Jerrah. You know good and well what I'm talkin' about."

"I really don't." Playing dumb was hopeless, but I was committed to the lie. It didn't occur to me at the time, but looking back on it, I didn't want Missy to be ashamed of me.

"Come off it. You've been stalkin' Rodrigo Suarez. I've seen the tweets. Everbody knows it was you."

"I ain't been stalkin' anyone. Did you get a load of all the things that that punk-ass said about me?"

"Some of it wasn't so nice, but can you blame him?"

"I sure as hell can."

"You accused him of stealin' your novel, Jerrah. Do you realize how nutty that sounds?"

"Welp, Jerry," I said to myself, "May as well just fess up to it. No need to go easy on the guy. Can't let him steal all your friends, too."

Out loud, I said, "Thing is, it ain't so nutty."

"What novel?" she said, raising her voice to a near-shout. "You don't write novels."

"How do you know?"

"Because I know. What're you gonna tell me next, Jerrah? That you do brain surgery in your spare time?"

"Well, that would be downright ridiculous, wouldn't it?"

"That's my point."

"Listen, Missy, I know it sounds insane, but I'm tellin' you: I wrote that novel and Rodrigo Suarez stole it from me."

"Do you even hear yourself?"

"Loud and clear."

"What did that boy ever do to you?"

"Sounds like you're the one with the hearin' problem."

"I'm only gonna ask one more time, Jerrah."

I sighed and looked her straight in the eyes. "He's a fuckin' fraud, a fake, a phony. Jesus, Missy. What more do you need to know?"

"That's not true."

"He ain't even Indian. Shit, he ain't even from Latin America. He's from the Midwest. He's a goddamn con artist."

"He explained the whole Indian thing."

"Yeah, by lyin' even more."

"No, Jerrah, there's a huge history of Native Americans gettin', like, sorted and classified accordin' to blood quantum, like animals, like dogs. What you're doin' is race science and honestly I'm disappointed in you."

And there it was. For over twenty years I had been listening to Missy's admonitions without a single care, but this one set me off. "I don't give a fuck. Stay disappointed, then."

With that, Missy rolled her eyes and spun around dramatically. We haven't spoken since. I saw her around town or campus every now and again, but she refused to make eye contact and I kept on moving. I still carry around a picture from our grad school days, though it's frayed and faded from so much travel. There's the gang, piled into a booth at BT's, wearing clothes that perfectly identify the era: droopy polos and corduroy jackets, all in the turn-of-the-century coloring that manages to look bright and pale all at once. Missy and I are next to each other. Her arm is around my waist and mine is around her shoulder. She has a huge, goofy grin and looks like she's about to plant a kiss on my cheek. She's young and skinny with wavy hair. I'm smiling, too, maybe with a bit of arrogance or irreverence. But the smile was genuine. Missy had a way of getting that kind of thing out of difficult people.

I do surely miss her.

# 19

Missy's plan to bring Rodrigo to Radford in conjunction with his Virginia Tech reading didn't work out. She sent a dejected email to the department list explaining that his agent wanted Radford to provide the normal fee even though Tech was the primary host and we simply couldn't afford such a large sum. A bunch of people responded to the list mourning the bad news and praising Missy for her effort.

I certainly wasn't surprised about Rodrigo being a greedy bastard. It fit everything I knew about the guy. There was a lot of money to be made flattering the delusions of educated people. Rodrigo was running a scam on the entire humanities.

I was curious about what he charged, but couldn't ask Missy. His website didn't list any prices. I reckon that it would have been considered tacky. My visit to the site wasn't a total waste, though. On the page with his upcoming reading schedule, I noticed the entry just below Virginia Tech: Bluefield State College.

Seeing Bluefield State on the list wasn't just any old surprise; it was something closer to a miracle. Famous writers–famous anybodies–rarely visit Bluefield. And rarely does an enemy so generously serve himself up on a platter.

At first I didn't believe what I saw. It seemed too good to be true. And I couldn't make sense of somebody like Rodrigo going to Bluefield State. Choosing Bluefield State over Radford was like choosing Radford over UVA.

Besides all that, why the hell would Bluefield State invite Rodrigo in the first place?

I emailed an old buddy who worked in the physical plant over there. He knew all the goings-on around campus. Apparently Bluefield State had come into a bundle of federal money owing to its status as an HBCU despite its mostly white student base. The school is located across the tracks in an old Black neighborhood filled with the descendants of coalminers and railroaders brought in at the turn of the twentieth century. Somewhere along the way, white students began to outnumber the Black. Bluefield State kept the HBCU designation, though, and was obliged to spend a small fortune on multicultural programming. I'll give those rascals all due credit: Rodrigo was the perfect choice. They'd have never doled out five figures to the real author of *Coyote Road*.

Once my amusement wore off, I started thinking on a plan. Yeah, Rodrigo's appearance in Bluefield was a damn fine bit of luck, but I couldn't screw this thing up. It's not every day that a vulture tries to feast on the living.

I picked up the phone and a gruff voice answered after the fifth ring.

"Jer."

"How you doin', Terrah?"

"Not too bad, all in all. Still above ground, anyhow. You?"

"That about covers it." I lowered my voice, as if we were at a party, talking in person. "Listen, I need a huge favor."

# 20

I didn't trust my memory–it wasn't too weak, but too strong–so I decided to do a bit of recon. I set my alarm early the next Saturday and rushed through my usual morning routine: a spot of coffee left over from the prior night, a smoke, a shit, and a quick shower. I was on the road a little past noon.

Spring was still a while away and as I merged onto 81 I felt entrapped by the balding mountains. They were surrounded by the usual overcast the color of undyed cotton and faded ink. Some people find it beautiful. To me it was a miserable scene. I always thought that folks around these parts get meaner during the winter. I had no way of testing the theory, but I remember how the outside gloom seeped through every crack and crevice in our rickety house in the middle of autumn. It felt tailor-made for meanness. I was feeling pretty goddamn mean myself.

The mountains grew larger and more depressing as I rounded north. Maybe it was the long line of truck stops peddling cheap gas from Fort Chiswell all the way to Wytheville that soured my mood. I always saw those low, sprawling buildings with enormous parking lots as a blight on the landscape. I never complained about cheap gas, though.

By the time I was in Bland County, I'd forgotten about Rodrigo and reconnaissance and everything else. My mind was on the K'iche' village I'd lived in, surrounded by an altogether different kind of mountains. Lush and warm and green year-round. Filled with fauna way more exotic than bobcats and black bears. Even when the sky was gray it felt bright.

What kind of person was I there, in that remote village, shuttling crafts and textiles to the big city? That person was still inside of me, somewhere, but I couldn't find him. He was like a mysterious creature who lived in a faraway, foreign body. I spent way too much time searching for that creature. And the more I searched, the farther away I moved from my own sense of self.

One morning, I was sitting on a stool outside the village's little store, sipping on a lukewarm Fanta, when Doña Justina showed up with a toddler against her hip. Doña Justina was super thin, but appeared to have no trouble carrying the extra weight.

"Who's that?" I asked in K'iche', nodding toward the child.

"Your K'iche', Mister," she said in English. "Very good."

Doña Justina always answered in English whenever I practiced my K'iche', even when encouraging me to keep learning the language. I watched as she bought a candy, the child's eyes sparkling with anticipation, and then swirled back onto the street, giving me a slight nod on her way out. She cut quite a figure in the dreary town.

Her hair was still jet black, which made a lovely contrast to her vibrant blouse. The colors of her ensemble fit the surroundings: green flora, yellow carambola, beige houses, blue horizons, red agricultural land.

She was moseying to some kind of destination. Everyone here, I realized, my ass fixed on a stool for no particular reason, had a destination in mind. Didn't matter where. Could be a community kitchen, could be California. More than anything, this shared idea of destiny kept the community alive and together. I tried my best to make sense of it, but I was foreign to the idea. I suppose Doña Justina knew that I wasn't yet ready for her language.

This memory weighed on my mind as I zoomed up the interstate to Bluefield. Truth is, I wasn't only furious with Rodrigo. I had taken forever to write a novel. I never tried to advance my career. I was content getting drunk and chasing skirt. I allowed myself to get punked by some social-climbing lowlife.

Well, whatever. Rodrigo's sorry ass was going to pay for all of it.

The tunnel under East River Mountain snapped me back into the present. "Focus, Jerry, focus," I repeated to myself. I had a big job ahead of me. I could work out all the existential crap after I dealt with Rodrigo.

I emerged in West Virginia and saw nothing that would improve my mood. It was even gloomier on the other side of the mountain. I didn't have a plan, so I drove to my childhood house. The entire town was to the right of the highway. The mountain ran along the opposite side. It was a nice view: the ridges and valleys on the Virginia side gave way to shorter hills pressed more closely together on the way north into West Virginia. This afternoon the mountain seemed more like a wall meant to protect the town against distant tomfoolery than a natural geographic feature.

I arrived at my old house, wondering why I went there in the first place. It had been empty for a few years. Mama stayed in it until she died and then I sold it for enough to buy a few dozen pitchers. The people who bought it had either died or moved away. I wasn't curious enough to find out. I doubted anyone would live in the house again. The clapboard siding was half-rotted and the roof badly needed to be replaced. A lot of the nearby houses looked empty, too. I could have gone inside, but instead I headed on to Bluefield State.

The school is in an older part of town, on the West Virginia side. You have to cross a bunch of railroad tracks to get there. When I was a kid, the bridge spanning those tracks had sidewalks and a concrete railing lined with thin arches. But a while ago they built a new bridge that looks like any other road. From the middle of the bridge, the town is dense and actually looks busy if you don't pay too much attention. Bluefield State is about a quarter-mile to the right. The road continues on to McDowell County. There's a back way where you can leave campus by driving through a down-and-out neighborhood and then crossing the tracks near downtown, which is filled with empty buildings and nightclubs (including a defunct gay bar that was the subject of constant ridicule in my childhood). Bluefield was supposedly a happening town back in the heyday of coal, but it was long dead by the time I was old enough to notice. From downtown, it wasn't too far to 460, which could take me down to Tazewell or up to Princeton depending on the situation. It wasn't too far from the town's few hotels, either.

All in all, not a terrible place to carry out some retribution.

# 21

I was restless while awaiting Rodrigo's arrival to the New River Valley. Now, don't get me wrong, I sure as shit wasn't going to his reading at Virginia Tech, or whatever else he'd be doing over the course of two days, but we'd be heading for Bluefield at roughly the same time, so I intended to keep an eye on his movements.

Missy made the job easier. She kept updating the department list, setting up a caravan of students and faculty for the reading, with a discussion group to follow. It never surprised me that she did so well in this industry. I could see it coming ever since the days when I tried to court one of her students.

Anyway, I carried on as normal. Given the fact that I'd been doxed, it struck me as a terrible idea to be anywhere near Rodrigo. I wasn't worried about getting busted in Bluefield. Any nitwit can get away with crime there. Hell, Radford isn't really any more civilized, but the faculty grapevine can be deadly if you're not careful. I knew how to move through Bluefield. Should any suspicion fall my way, I was confident that I'd be able to explain my whereabouts.

On the Monday after my recon trip, I was in class looking and sounding the same as I always did, not that the students would have noticed any changes. We were doing a unit on rational claims: X is/is not Y. It was a simple concept, but year after year a bunch of students missed the point, coming up with junk like "freedom isn't free" or "marijuana isn't illegal." No matter how slowly I explained that the purpose of the upcoming paper was to apply evidence and reason to common wisdom, the students saw the unit as a word game. Some of them insisted on being stubbornly, idiotically wrong about the meaning of evidence and reason. I half-expected to see them one day doing cable news analysis.

I was trying to explain why spelling out assumptions is a good idea when a squeaky sound emitted from the back of the room, low and steady before escalating into something akin to a note from an untuned trombone. About half the students looked at their desks and snickered. A few others grinned stupidly. The rest looked annoyed. They knew the routine. The peculiar event happened at least once a week.

I sighed. "Chick-Fil-A for breakfast again, Russ?"

A kid in the back-right corner grinned and held up and empty wrapper. "Yes, sir. Those chicken biscuits are dope."

This student, Russ, would bring Chick-Fil-A biscuits to class and then gleefully let it rip. The first time it happened, everyone laughed, including myself. The second time was more restrained. The third time, I began to wonder if the kid was mentally challenged.

It turned out he wasn't, not by traditional metrics, at least. He was just uncouth and shameless. Probably in need of more attention, too, which he got plenty of thanks to the orchestral notes exuding from his asshole. The students seated near him made a production of moving away even though they were clearly flattered. One girl in particular kept sitting in front of him, knowing what was coming and then acting mortified when it came. She was tiny and fake blonde and always wore sorority letters which I couldn't decipher because I never bothered to learn that stuff. It struck me as likely that Russ would end up in her pants.

This was supposed to be a normal Monday, and I was supposed to be the same old instructor, so I hid my agitation. I wanted to ask Russ when the routine would get old, but I already knew the answer: when he ceased to be rewarded for it.

"Okay, Russ," I said, maybe showing a bit of agitation. "We get it: you love chicken biscuits."

More snickering.

Before Russ had a chance to cock up his leg one more time, I decided to try a different tack.

"How's this for a possible topic?" I said. "Farting in class is . . . ." I waved two fingers in a circle to solicit their feedback. Once they stopped giggling, the answers came quickly. I wrote the first ten on the board: gross, rude, awesome, hilarious, inappropriate, disgusting, immature, ballsy, disrespectful, insane. Some of the words were close to synonymous, but had gradations of meaning that I pushed the students to identify. Even Russ quit farting around and contributed a few not entirely idiotic comments. We spent the rest of class exploring the fine-tuned rhetorical possibilities of flatulence. It wasn't a normal day, but it was abnormal in all the right ways.

The morning was a good reminder that teaching could be fun and rewarding. Normally I got reminders of the meager pay and the monotony. I didn't think about Rodrigo until returning to my office and realized how much I needed a break from anything to do with him. He was everywhere, in both the physical and abstract. The motherfucker was in my inbox, my favorite bookstores, my social media feeds, my dreams and memories. And soon he'd be strutting around the campuses I'd known since childhood. More than anything, he was stuck inside my frontal cortex and I knew that in order to survive I would have to get rid of him.

# PART III

# 1

Welp, this is where things get interesting. You'll have to bear with me as I sort the details. Long story short: everything went more or less according to plan. At last I got to meet Rodrigo. You know how they say that it's a bad idea to meet a famous person because you'll inevitably be disappointed? The opposite was true with Rodrigo: I wasn't disappointed at all; our meeting made me like him a little better.

Let me start from the beginning.

Rodrigo, as expected, filled up an entire auditorium in Tech's student center. Half the English professors probably forced their students to go, but the wider interest was legitimate. The guy could draw a crowd in ways I'd never be able to, no matter what I published. I considered going. I could have slipped in without being seen, but it would have been too painful, knowing that I should be the one onstage. I mostly wanted to hear him try and explain his fake identity, but I knew nobody would bring it up. That kind of stuff was reserved for online media. You didn't challenge a man's honesty in person, in public, with hundreds of spectators ready to take his side. You'd become the person with questionable values.

I followed along on Facebook and Twitter. Rodrigo was a smash, of course. People seemed to love exactly what I hated about him: his arrogance, his contempt, his hokey cadence, his inane social commentary. I couldn't imagine that Bluefield had enough people who would entertain his bullshit. But what did it matter to him? He got paid just the same.

He would spend the next day and night in Blacksburg, visiting classrooms, doing some radio, dining and drinking with dozens of professors dying to be in the presence of fame. I wanted to get out ahead of him. The night of his reading, I headed over to Bluefield without telling anyone.

I knew Rodrigo would stay one night in Bluefield. No more, no less. If it were up to him, I'm sure he'd get in and out lickety-split. He didn't have a choice, though. A million little obligations were likely written into his contract. Host colleges liked to get their money's worth out of these bigwig visitors. Besides, the closest airport was in Roanoke, an hour-and-a-half away, minimum. Incidentally, it was the airport serving Blacksburg. I figured Rodrigo's agent had already gotten an earful for putting his stops in the wrong order.

Basically, I had two days to fine-tune the plan. I didn't waste any time once I got to Bluefield. I drove straight to Terry's house and banged on the front door.

"Jer?" he answered, wearing boxers and a droopy white T-shirt. "What're you doin' here?"

"Remember I said I might need a huge favor?" He nodded lazily. "Yeah, it's about that time."

# 2

I sat in a tattered knit armchair while Terry rifled around his kitchen.

"Sorry, buddy," he called out. "Ain't got no more liquor. Just beer."

I highly doubted that Terry didn't have liquor squirreled away somewhere. It wasn't like him to be without at least a bottle or an emergency stash. It wasn't anything worth arguing over, so I told him beer was fine. He shuffled back into the living room and plopped on a couch across from me, the same one that was in the house when we were children. Foam stuffing was sticking out from various tears in the fabric. The carpet hadn't been changed since our childhood. It was either brown or beige depending on the origin of the stain. I vaguely remembered the carpet being a burnt orange way back when. It was covered with empty beer cans and food wrappers. For all I knew, Terry hadn't cleaned since his parents died. It was hard to tell because nobody cleaned when his parents were alive, either. Not that the hovel I grew up in was much better.

He said, “Now tell me again what it is you’re fixin’ to do.”

I repeated the plan, again without going into any detail. Terry lit a cigarette and kept quiet for a little while. I didn’t rush him.

“And whaddya need me for?” he said finally.

“I need your help baggin’ the guy.”

“I don’t know, Jer. I’m tryin’ to stay out of trouble with the law.”

“I get it, man, but this is an easy job.” By using the word “job,” I hinted that there would be something in it for Terry. He picked up on the hint.

“Tell me more.”

I held up a pill bottle and shook it.

Terry squinted. “What’s that?”

“Perc, Oxy, Vicodin. Forty of ‘em.” I wasn’t into that stuff, but they were a damn good currency in Bluefield—and Radford, for that matter. Over the years, I’d collected whatever I could from prescriptions. Nobody ever suspected me of shopping because I spread out my doctor visits. A few minor surgeries over the years boosted my inventory. Some of the pills were well over a decade old. Maybe they were expired, but nobody would know the difference.

Terry’s eyes bulged in amazement. “Count me in,” he said.

# 3

We agreed that nabbing Rodrigo was best done after his event. Even if we could get to him beforehand, it didn't seem like a good idea to have a few hundred people wondering where the hell he was at. When the festivities ended, and he had been dropped off at his hotel, it would be hours before anyone noticed that he was missing.

Finding his hotel wouldn't be a problem. For a fancy guest like Rodrigo, there weren't many options. Terry and I could find out with a few phone calls. As we ran through the details, I could tell that Terry was warming up to the operation. I hadn't told him my specific grievances, but made it clear that Rodrigo was a major-league prick, the kind of guy Terry would enjoy slapping around.

I crashed on the couch and woke up next morning to Terry frying eggs in the kitchen. He was clanging around and whistling. The kitchen segued right into the living room, so it sounded like he was rapping a skillet right next to my head. I dragged myself up and stumbled to the coffee machine. It was empty.

"Goddamn, man," I said, "don't you drink coffee?"

"I'm tryin'a get healthier."

I looked at Terry's doughy midsection and shook my head. "It ain't coffee that's makin' you fat."

"Yeah, but that shit gives me the shakes. I don't like walkin' around feelin' nervous."

"You worried about our thing?"

"Nah."

"Good."

"My part is easy. You're the one who should feel nervous."

"I ain't, though. That's the thing: I just need a bit of time with the guy."

"Well . . . shouldn't be much of a problem."

After we ate–reluctantly on my part, as I kept staring at all the grease stains and crusty dishes on Terry's counter–we went out for a dry run. I looked around as we walked to Terry's old F-150. The place hadn't changed, except it had gotten worse. The small wooden houses were pocked with rot and slightly misshapen from decades of wind and snow. It didn't look like anyone used the court where we once played basketball. The rims had no nets and the asphalt was cracked into dozens of little hexagons and trapezoids. Nobody was out walking. Nobody ever did. Kids used to run around, but they'd all grown up and moved away or else, like Terry, became the next installment of the same generation. The neighborhood felt abandoned. Over the years it had gone from working class to indigent.

The rest of town wasn't better. The two elementary schools looked exactly the same as they did forty years ago–like shit. The old funeral home near downtown was the only building that suggested prosperity. It had been renovated and was kept in good condition. The churches seemed to be doing okay, as well. I saw a lot of rebel flags on cars and US flags on houses. Really, there wasn't much else to see: railroad crossings, naked hills, stumpy buildings, convenience stores. I reckon that at the beginning of summer, when Virginia Creeper was growing all over everything and the wildflowers were in bloom, the town would look better, maybe even pleasant, but Bluefield didn't have a summer climate. The mountains provided the area with plenty of beauty and they could also turn that beauty into an unlimited backdrop of gloom. Then you got to the old part of town where there was still enough coal to fill hundreds of Norfolk & Southern boxcars waiting behind squat stone walls dusted in soot.

In different circumstances, we'd have gone around visiting, but I wasn't supposed to be in town, so I wouldn't even be getting out of the car. No big deal, really. I didn't care to visit anyone. I wouldn't have minded seeing Slop Bucket, I guess, but he'd made good of himself and would be at the office. Mostly Terry and I just wasted time because we didn't need to know anything other than where Rodrigo would be sleeping and that was easy to find out.

I was still curious about the details of my history with the guy. It fascinated me that somebody who had ripped me off was coming to the place where I had grown up without having the slightest interest in anything to do with me. Where would I go in Bluefield? What might appeal to me? How would I move through town? None of it mattered. Rodrigo didn't fit in Bluefield and yet Rodrigo owed his success to the town.

And could Rodrigo maybe sense that this out-of-the-way place was at least partly responsible for his success? Where were the hosts going to take him to eat? Macado's? They were practically begging the guy to make fun of them on Twitter. He'd cash the check and then complain about all the yokels trying to steal his valor.

I have no special fondness for my hometown, but it seemed downright insulting to allow that sort of thing to happen.

# 4

We sat in the parking lot of the Quality Inn, nestled into the base of East River Mountain. It was a typical roadside motel that had changed ownership a million times since it first opened as a Holiday Inn back when I was a kid, but it was about the best in town. There were a handful of decent chain hotels in Princeton, the next town up in West Virginia, but I knew the Bluefield State people wouldn't put up Rodrigo in one of them. It was a decent-sized drive and, besides, they wouldn't want Rodrigo to see the strip clubs parked next to the interstate. They would want him to think of the region as quaint or rustic, not as vulgar. I wouldn't be doing much to help their effort.

Terry had parked at the back of the hotel, right at the edge of the woods. It was about as close as a place could get to being perfect for an abduction. There was a small TV station next door. Beyond that, the building was isolated, with a mountain on one side and a highway on the other.

"Right there," I said, pointing to a glass door leading to the back lot. "Can you get'm out from there?"

"I reckon so."

"I'll be waitin' right next to it in the car."

"Mmm hmm."

Terry seemed nonchalant to the point of indifference. I was growing worried. "Look, man, you ain't gotta do this if you don't want to."

"Nah, it's fine," he said as if I were asking him to pass the remote.

"You feelin' good about it?"

He shrugged. "Yeah. Sure."

It occurred to me that Terry might not have a single idea of what he was doing. I wasn't dealing with a seasoned CIA operative here, just some country boy motivated by a handful of pills he would either sell or snort.

"You got your plan made out?" I said, trying not to sound unconfident.

"You even sure he's stayin' here?"

"Not yet. But I'll call and ask for him. Ninety-nine percent sure he'll be here, though."

"And you know what time he's comin' in for the night?"

"More or less." Now I was beginning to worry about my own preparation. "I figure we'll shoot for about ten-thirty, eleven, show up an hour earlier or so. He won't be out any later, but I think it'll be too early for'm to sleep."

"Asleep, awake, it don't make a shit to me."

"Yeah, but showin' up too late's liable to cause trouble."

"Could be."

I knew that Terry was lackadaisical because he wasn't concerned about failing or getting caught. This was a risky job in terms of the law, but pretty cut-and-dry from an execution standpoint. I wasn't as convinced, so I decided to press a bit. "How you gon' get to his room?"

"Won't be a problem."

"How?"

"Them night clerks are all junkies–or else know plenty of 'em."

"So?"

"So you got any more of them pills?"

I figured that was coming and I did have more pills, actually. I was nervous to say so, though, because I didn't want Terry thinking I had held out on him. Then again, I had no other choice.

"Yeah," I admitted.

"How many?"

"Ten."

He knew I was lying and he also knew that I understood ten to be more than enough for the job. My stock was running low, but I wasn't about to admit it: Terry had good reason to behave if he thought I had a big supply.

# 5

In the end, Terry was right not to be worried. Rodrigo's disappearance got a fair amount of press, but nobody ever mentioned Terry's name. People knew him as the kind of guy who might pull some crazy shit, but Bluefield was filled with guys of similar character. Not even Sam Spade would think to connect Terry to Rodrigo.

The night before the big event, I slept on Terry's couch again, less nervous this time, and woke up the next morning earlier than normal. Terry was still conked out in his room, so I made myself coffee and opened my laptop. I checked email first, a longtime habit. I deleted everything new to my inbox—I could tell at a glance if there was anything that would interest me, a rare occurrence—and then headed to Twitter. I had quit posting after getting doxed, which somehow made me even more addicted. The Tech visit didn't produce any negative comments that I could find, so I navigated elsewhere to avoid the praise.

After a while, Terry shuffled out of his room and sat next to me. He glanced at my screen.

"You doin' that Twitter shit?"

"Kinda. I just lurk."

He shook his head as if I'd just announced that I like to fuck poodles. Terry wouldn't use Twitter on principle. He didn't like any social media. I suppose he thought it was inviting other people into his business, and he wasn't exactly wrong. Terry was an old-fashioned guy in general. It was a miracle he even had Wi-Fi.

He didn't have to explain any of this stuff to me. I understood his mentality. It didn't have anything to do with agreeing or disagreeing with his decisions; I know how the man's brain operates, that's all. He didn't know shit about college or close reading or literary criticism and he could still explain in great detail why I behave the way I do at my job. Terry and I were exactly the same and yet we had nothing in common.

"You ready for tonight?" I said.

His lips twisted into a thoughtful pose. "Yep. Just gotta be quick and careful."

"You know how you're gonna get'm from his room to the parking lot?"

He held a palm at mouth level, parallel to the ground. "You said he was yay big?"

"That's about right."

"I'll get'm down."

"I don't want you to hurt the guy."

"I ain't intendin' to hurt'm. It ain't gonna be pleasant, though. You understand that, right?"

"Right. Just don't bash his head in or nothin' like that."

"You want'm lookin' pretty for you, huh?"

"Fuck you."

"C'mon," he laughed, patting my knee. "Let's get into somethin'."

I didn't like the sound of that. "Somethin'" could mean just about anything, most of it no good. The last thing I needed was to get into trouble the day of the operation.

I offered to drive and Terry didn't object. The way I saw it, if I was driving then I could at least minimize the chance of being pulled over. I could also steer toward places that were less likely to involve either law or disorder.

Terry suggested getting hot dogs at the Dairy Queen and that sounded like a fine idea. I supposed it wouldn't do any harm to load up on some protein. The Dairy Queen used split-top Heiner's buns, buttered and seared, and you won't find a better restaurant dog anywhere. I didn't worry about anyone recognizing me. The place was empty. I stuck my face in a magazine just to be sure. Terry then wanted to stop by the ABC for some whiskey, but I didn't like the idea. I suggested bringing home some beer, instead.

I headed to the Short Stop–it was now Graham Mart but everyone still called it Short Stop–and waited in the car while Terry ran inside. He didn't return for around ten minutes.

"Sorry 'bout that," he said, swinging into the passenger seat. "I got to chattin' with some of the boys. I was waitin' for you to come join us."

"You know I can't afford to be seen."

Terry gave me a half-smile. I knew he thought I was being paranoid and maybe I was. Sitting in a parking lot while a bunch of people walked by didn't help.

"Our hotdogs done got cold," I complained.

"We can microwave 'em."

I was going below the speed limit. With an unregistered Glock in the glove box and a 12-pack of beer on the floorboard, getting stopped would be a bad turn of events. Used to be that it wouldn't concern me much. I'd grown up with most of the police force, but I wasn't a local anymore, not really. Terry wasn't any safer. He used to do odd jobs for Pearce, but Pearce had died a few years ago. The new generation of cop had less imagination.

I could see Terry's impatience. He was tapping an index finger against his thigh and kept looking at me.

"Whatsa matter?" he said finally. "You got a baseball stuck underneath the gas pedal?"

"I ain't takin' no chances."

"Fine. You're still drivin' too slow."

"Jesus, man, we'll be home in two minutes."

"Shit, I could run faster'n you're going."

"Shut the fuck up."

"I ain't even kiddin'."

"Oh yeah? Show me. I'll let you off right here and go the same speed I been drivin'. It's faster'n you think."

"Do it."

I stopped the car. "Be my guest."

As soon as he shut the door, I slammed the accelerator and the Altima jumped forward with a squeal. I had no intention of stopping or turning around. I could see Terry in the rearview mirror, looking hotter than Hades.

I was settling onto the couch with my hotdogs, fresh out of the microwave, when Terry walked in.

"Bastard," he muttered, snatching the Dairy Queen bag from the arm of the couch.

After lunch, Terry was restless. I told him to run around all he liked, that I intended to take a nap and get my head straight. He didn't end up leaving and we watched TV the rest of the afternoon. I nodded off a few times, but I was too antsy for proper sleep.

Somewhere around nine, we started getting ready. I prepared an overnight bag and Terry stuffed gloves and a balaclava into his coat pockets. We drove separately. If all went well, Terry would be returning home alone. Me and Rodrigo would be taking a drive.

Terry parked on one end of the lot with a view of the front entrance. I parked on the opposite side. I chain-smoked and browsed Twitter while we waited.

# 6

It was a cold and clear night and I could see a spattering of stars spread above the crest of the mountain. I might have enjoyed the view in different circumstances. The wait was driving me crazy. My phone dinged and I saw a message from Terry.

"This pussy coming or not?"

He was going crazy, too. It didn't make me feel any better. I needed Terry to be confident. The fact that he was itching for action meant the opposite. The longer he sat around, the more anxious he became.

I texted back, "Keep still he's coming."

It was getting late and I worried that somebody had roped Rodrigo into staying out for drinks. That could lead to a bunch of other problems. "86 the plan if he's not alone," I added.

"OK."

And so we kept on waiting. I wanted to turn the car on for heat, but it was too risky. Hotel employees are always on the lookout for shady individuals in the parking lot. I guess I'd grown soft over the years. When I was young, cold weather didn't affect me much. I don't really remember noticing the cold at all, to be honest. Recently, though, I started paying attention to chilly spells in April and May. They put me in a foul mood. My body was changing for the worse and anyway it had been a long while since I screwed around outside in freezing weather. I wanted to retreat into a more innocent version of myself that got up to no good without worrying about the consequences. I never made anything of my life, but I had no desire to trade a dead-end job for prison. I was already on thin ice at work because of the online feud with Rodrigo. My chair and dean (and God knows who else) were none too happy about all the complaints they had received. Tenure sure would have come in handy, but it wouldn't be available no matter how long I worked at Radford.

I reckon it was mostly my fault, although Radford's the kind of place that drags everyone into mediocrity. All colleges do, really; they just have different notions of what counts as mediocre. They like to call it institutional culture. They'll get you to conform, one way or another. That means you can't go around disrupting your place in the hierarchy. I was what my employer wanted me to be. No more, no less. It was delusional to think all those years that I was my own man. I was a sales rep pitching an overpriced product to a bunch of apathetic customers. Becoming successful like Rodrigo would have fucked up the entire market.

What had I ever accomplished, then? I was okay with women. I made more money than most of my childhood friends. I didn't live in some clapboard pigsty. That's all well and good by Bluefield standards. Not by real standards, though. I was on the bottom rung of my profession:

an untenured instructor at an obscure regional comprehensive university. I'd never seen my name in print until the government started putting arrest records online. When it comes right down to it, getting ripped off by a social media conman was my greatest achievement.

A set of headlights cut across the parking lot, interrupting my self-pity. A car pulled up to the loading area in front of the entrance. I furiously tapped at my knee. The car idled for a short while before the passenger door opened. I leaned forward to get a good look. The oblique light from the carport cast the passenger in silhouette as he stepped onto the pavement, but there was no doubt about his identity.

It was Rodrigo. He was alone.

# 7

With the headlights off, I inched the car to the back exit. I parked in front of the door and kept the engine running. About ten minutes later, Terry appeared from around the corner. He winked at me and went inside. He had managed to get a working key card for the door.

I began rehearsing what I would say to Rodrigo. Pretty soon I was running through angry, elaborate monologues. I had wanted to get my hands on the bastard for a long time, but it never occurred to me just how much I had on my mind.

My adrenaline gave way to a feeling of dread. What was taking Terry so long? And why was I so stupid to have trusted him in the first place? Terry wasn't some kind of criminal mastermind, some smooth enforcer like you see in mafia movies. He was a guy who viewed lawbreaking as a mixture of work and recreation. Terry probably didn't intend for it to happen, but he was at the vanguard of

Appalachia's post-coal economy. So I had to give him at least a little bit of credit. Kidnapping a celebrity was above his rank, though.

And what about my rank? Was this sort of activity out of place for an English instructor? It might look like it at first, but I'd argue the opposite: professors are some of the biggest goons you'll ever meet. Their weapons are language. If you don't think that nuance and wordplay are dangerous, then you've never seen a decorated intellectual in action. They can screw up a lot of lives with some well-timed affect and dissimulation. It's hard to see because they're really good at carrying out indirect violence. But it happens. Trust me on that. I've seen plenty of motherfuckers taken out by card-carrying nerds with a fancy vocabulary. And the assassin primped and cringed the entire time like some anguished bystander.

So I guess you could say that I was prepared for my encounter with Rodrigo. Philosophically, anyway. My profession is all about territory and that shitbag had encroached onto mine with a tank battalion.

I saw movement out of the corner of my eye. A large, lumpy shadow appeared in the vestibule followed by the actual bodies of Terry and Rodrigo. Terry was behind him, trying to move him forward, but Rodrigo wasn't making it easy. He kept twisting and thrashing and Terry tried to control him with kicks and knocks to the back of his head. Stringy hair flew around from the bottom of Terry's balaclava. As they got close to the door, I saw that Rodrigo's hands were tied behind his back and there was a rolled-up pair of socks stuck in his mouth, held into place by two loops of duct tape.

Terry managed to push his captive to the open passenger door. Rodrigo was trying to scream, but the fabric muffled the sound. He kept flailing around. Terry hit him in the back of the head with the heel of his palm and said, "Sit the hell down." Terry finally got him into the seat. "Careful. He's a frisky little fucker," he panted before slamming the door and running back to his truck.

Rodrigo was still thrashing and flailing. His eyes seemed to be screaming "who are you?"

I gave him a big smile. "You might as well settle down, Mr. Suarez. Or should I call you Jason?" He thrashed even harder. His muffled screams became more desperate. I sped out of the parking lot. As I neared the highway, I patted Rodrigo's knee. "You may wanna shut the fuck up now. Ain't nobody comin' to save you."

# 8

I went west on 460, toward the Virginia line, which was about a mile away. I had no specific escape route. I had tried to think of one in advance but decided to go with instinct once Rodrigo was in my possession. I suppose that deep down I didn't believe it would actually happen.

Rodrigo had settled a bit. I kept looking in his direction. Terry had smacked him around pretty good: the skin surrounding his eyes was inflamed and covered in moisture. Red marks a finger wide streaked across his cheeks and the side of his neck. People sometimes look different in real life than they do online. Rodrigo looked the same: part nerd, part queer, part frat boy. I guess if you searched hard enough, you could find something unwhite about his features. It would require a lot of squinting. He had medium-brown hair, soft and wavy, which matched the color of his pupils. His complexion was clear and creamy; it didn't look like it would last long on a hot day in August.

A few miles down the road, he started up again. This time he wasn't having a tantrum. His eyes were bulging and he was rocking his head back and forth. I glared at him and kept on driving. He kept it up and I was about to give him a smack when I realized that his skin had a purplish undertone. When he began sniffing in rapid bursts I understood what was happening. I pulled to the shoulder and took the Glock out of my jacket pocket. I pointed it a few inches from his forehead and said, "A single goddamn word and I'll put one right in your eye." He nodded desperately.

I undid the duct tape, ripping a bunch of hairs off Rodrigo's scalp, and then pulled the sock out of his mouth. He swayed back and forth and heaved. For a second I thought he was fixing to vomit, but he held it in. I put the gun back in his face. "Remember what I told you."

I pulled back onto the highway and kept my speed between fifty and fifty-five. Rodrigo panted like an overheated quarter horse, but he kept quiet. The gun rested on my right thigh, where he couldn't miss it, in case he needed a reminder.

# 9

The night was conducive to driving, so I just drove. I skipped the exits to Bluefield and blew through Springville. When I saw the sign for Tazewell, I decided to get off the highway. For all I knew, the cops could be looking for us already.

The stars glistened brightly at this late hour and cold quickly seeped into the car whenever I cut down the heat. I took a right on a country road, winding through alternating patches of wood and farmland, eerie in the dim nighttime glow. I had a vague sense that I'd pulled onto Route 16, which would slowly take us up to an outpost called Bishop and then into West Virginia. These were some real backwoods and even if anyone was after us it would take them a while to navigate the boonies we winded through with deliberate impatience.

I wasn't only thinking about strategy. A strange force had overcome me and I was drawn into the backcountry, as if hostage to the whims of a self-driving car. I was alert but also in a state of semi-consciousness. I still didn't know what to do. A montage of possibilities fluttered through my mind; none of them stuck. I was focused on the dark narrow road, a morass of dips and twists, and periodically remembered that I wasn't on a joyride. If his hands weren't bound, Rodrigo probably could have snatched the gun from my lap.

We were near Bishop when I settled back into the present.

"Why'd you do it?" I said.

Rodrigo continued looking forward. I wasn't sure if he heard me, so I repeated the question, louder this time. He stayed quiet, but I could tell by the way his lips shifted that he heard me.

"I asked you a question," I said.

More silence.

I fixed my attention back on the road so as not to lose my temper. I had no specific plan for Rodrigo, but all along my main goal, my only goal, really, was to get answers. If I didn't get those answers, then the mission would be a failure no matter what else happened. I was about to pick up the gun and do things the hard way when I sensed that Rodrigo was looking at me. I returned his stare and raised my eyebrows.

"I don't know what you're talking about." Gone was the smarmy, self-important cadence he used on camera. He spoke softly and I might have detected some contrition in his voice.

I ran my thumb up and down the butt of the gun. "You must think I'm in the mood for more of your bullshit. I've had more'n enough of it, believe you me."

"Who are you?"

"You know good and goddamn well who I am."

"I have no idea who you are."

I wanted to tell him that I didn't always know myself, and that he suffered the same condition, but it didn't seem like a good time to get philosophical.

"You wanna take a guess?" I said.

"Why are you doing this to me?" I could hear tears inflecting his voice.

"You know why."

"Oh my God," he moaned. "Why do you think I know you?"

"You're the one who doxed me, ain't you?"

The whites of his eyes expanded. "Jesus Christ. I should have known."

"If it makes you feel better, I always took you for a dumb motherfucker."

"Of course it's you. Of course. I mean, I never thought it would come to this, that you'd, like, actually fucking show up and kidnap me. I didn't think you were that crazy. I just–"

"Kidnappin's the least of your concerns." I picked up the gun and waved it. "In fact, kidnappin's about the best outcome you can hope for."

# 10

A funny thing happened once Rodrigo and I got to talking: I started to hate him a tiny bit less. Now, don't get it confused. Just because I lost a smidgen of hatred didn't mean I intended to go easy on him. I still had to take care of business. Dealing with Rodrigo was the only way I could reclaim my life. I was expecting the hatred to intensify, that's all, so I had to readjust my mindset.

"Where are we?" he said.

"Just got into West Virginia. This is coal country. Or used to be, at least."

He didn't answer, so I got back to the point. "I wanna know how you did it."

"Did what?" He practically spit out the second word.

"Don't start playin' dumb with me again."

"I really don't know."

"How you stole my novel."

"You're still beating that dead horse?"

"Don't get smart with me, you thievin' little cocksucker, or I'll stop with the horse and start beatin' your ass, instead. Now tell me how you did it before I run out of patience."

"My God, you really believe it, don't you? I thought it was a bit or something. You know, some random trying to stir things up. You wouldn't believe how many weirdos are out there. But you–holy shit–you're convinced I really stole your novel."

I picked up the pistol and popped the side of his head. He began screaming and stamping his feet.

"Quit bein' a pussy," I said. He kept at it. "I told you already to shut the fuck up or I'm gonna put some force behind it next time."

He took down the volume but continued whimpering. I let him wind back down to silence.

"Look," he said finally. "There's obviously been a misunderstanding. Okay? Why don't you just let me go and we'll forget that any of this happened."

I let out an exaggerated chuckle. "That's a great idea. How far down the road do you figure I'll be before you're tellin' the story on Twitter?"

"I won't say anything, I swear."

"Oh, I know you ain't gonna say anything."

"I promise there's no need to do this."

I made like I was reaching for the gun. Rodrigo gasped and pressed himself against the door. "I wanna know how you did it," I said calmly. "Did you steal it from the cloud or whatever? Did an editor slip it to you? Did you hack into my computer?"

"I . . . I . . . didn't," he sobbed.

I grabbed his hair and shook violently, letting go so that his head smacked the window. "You dumb lyin' motherfucker. You're gonna tell me one way or another. But if you wanna do it the hard way, that's fine by me."

"But I didn't steal anything," he said.

"You stole an entire goddamn identity."

After a few seconds, he said, "Look, okay, I'll admit to that. Everybody does it. You think there's a writer anywhere in the world who hasn't embellished a past? Not a single writer is who they say they are."

"Nah, there are degrees. There's a difference between embellishin' and outright lyin'." It suddenly felt like I was in a classroom, debating students. "You're runnin' around pretendin' to be an Indian from Guatemala. That's some next-level shit."

"I don't think so." Now his voice was steady and slightly excitable, as if he were eager to finally have this debate. "Invention is invention. Yeah, there are degrees, but we're all guilty. Besides, I became what the audience wanted me to be. That's all I did."

"Cut the malarkey."

"It's not. You think readers want a story about migration from some generic Midwestern white kid?"

"You don't have to tell me twice. But they deserve at least a bit more respect than you've shown 'em. Not to mention what you owe me."

"Listen, dude. I didn't steal your novel. I'm serious. I don't know why you believe that."

My agitation returned. "You dense motherfucker. Jesus. Just when you start makin' a bit of sense, you go right back to lyin'."

"I don't know how I can possibly convince you, but I didn't steal your novel. I've never met you. I've never read anything by you. I've never heard of you. I just . . . this is all so terribly confusing."

I tapped the Glock and considered his denial.

# 11

The talking messed with my sense of space and time. We were still on Route 16, heading north, but I didn't know exactly where. I kept tapping the gun while thinking over Rodrigo's denial.

I was annoyed that his argument made sense. But I couldn't deny it. Writers don't just invent stories; they also invent personas, which can be more important than the stories they tell. Hell, I did it without even having been published. I was the aloof and carefree non-artist, too cynical for all the pageantry. I never made writing part of my public identity. Maybe I was embarrassed by my failures. Maybe I lacked enough status to brag. Maybe I didn't allow myself the title of "writer" until I was published, or published multiple times, or sold a certain amount of books, or got written up in *The New Yorker*. I don't fucking know. Whatever it was, I passed it off as disdain. I was too cool to care about all that high-fallutin' nonsense. There's very little space between sanctimony and indifference.

So I could empathize to a degree with Rodrigo for lying about his identity. We all lie about our identities. Yeah, there are levels to it and some people take it way too far, but I don't know where embellishment becomes a lie and when the lying becomes unethical. None of this stuff was an issue back in the K'iche' village. You were Indian or you were white. Nobody there had trouble situating me in the world and they had no confusion about who they were. Even when they left or had their land stolen, they tied their entire sense of being to a specific region. We didn't have that luxury in Virginia or Illinois or Florida or wherever. We descend from the conquerors, the takers, the settlers, and we'll never be able to root ourselves in the same way no matter how much we chirp about homespun values. That's why Appalachian Studies never made sense to me and why my friends and I treated Bluefield as a way station to be destroyed rather than a homeland to be protected and cherished. We had no understanding of community. We had no notion of the sacred. We only reacted to unseen legacies of violence.

But Rodrigo's lying was on a whole different level. He wasn't claiming to be Appalachian or Latino. He was taking from people who had no trouble with ethnic categories. These problems belonged to the settler, not the native. The native didn't deserve Rodrigo's baggage.

None of it mattered in the end because the main issue was theft and there was no way to justify it. Bullshitting about the past was more or less accepted, even encouraged, but stealing material was still unacceptable. Or it was supposed to be, anyway. I started wondering if that was really the case. I used to browse *The Chronicle of Higher Education* in the faculty lounge and it seemed that every other week there was some new allegation of plagiarism.

What happened to the accused? I didn't follow each story, but the way I remember it, most of them got off scot-free. Well, good for them. I wasn't going to accept it in any circumstance. Somebody has to uphold professional standards.

I didn't know what to make of Rodrigo's denial. I sure as hell didn't believe him, but was pretty impressed by his skill at lying. He didn't show the usual tells: stuttering, fidgeting, passive language, twitchy eyes. He was defensive in a way that felt appropriate given the seriousness of my allegation. There was something about him I couldn't wave away, something that felt deeply familiar. He wasn't what I expected. I mean, he was, in the sense of being a pretty boy preening for attention, but his personality was different. His private personality, not the one he dresses in for the internet. He wasn't all con artist, for example. He could raise a point and defend it. There was a brain somewhere behind the gibberish. That discovery threw me off. I could have whooped up on him a bit more, but I didn't get the sense it would make me feel any better. And I doubted it would get him talking about *Coyote Road.* He was adamant that he wrote it and I didn't figure he'd crack under the type of torture I was willing to dish out.

I glanced over. Rodrigo's head was resting against the window and he stared into the darkness outside. The side of his face was still ruddy with moisture. He looked at peace despite the situation. I got the sense that he was chiding himself for not hating me as much as he ought to. I had to admit that I felt some kind of affinity for him, which suddenly made me hate the motherfucker even more.

# 12

I'd been driving longer than I had intended. We were deep into the hills. Some overcast had formed and so an even greater darkness filled the slopes and crevices. I'd been in this country before—I'd been in all the country of Southern West Virginia and Southwest Virginia at some point, joyriding and looking for trouble—but it was unfamiliar enough to where I couldn't quite locate myself on a map. A rectangular green sign came into view, announcing that it was two miles to War. I was an hour from Bluefield—longer, probably, because of the dark—and over two hours from Radford. I wasn't returning to Terry's house—I'd be taking a long break from Terry—and didn't want to risk sleeping in a parking lot or on the side of the road. It's an invitation for cops to poke around trying to snag an easy DUI. I'd definitely gone far enough.

I took the next side road to the right and began scouting places to stop. There wasn't much, just some homesteads and shacks, all of them dark. About a mile on, I came across a small building with a large parking lot. It was an old autobody shop. I pulled in and saw that the place was abandoned. The lot was half gravel and the squat cinder building had cracks zigzagging from ground to ceiling. As I swung the car around, I could see a rusted sign hanging above the door: Swetnam's Foreign and Domestic Service. The windows in both garage doors were broken. It didn't look like the place had been open in five or ten years. I drove around to the back, fully out of view of the street. The lot backed up to a hillside. Nobody was around to interrupt us.

"Where are you taking me?" Rodrigo said.

"I don't know."

I put the car in park and turned off the headlights. I kept the engine running. Rodrigo's left knee jerked up and down. I'm pretty sure he'd have run for it if his hands were free. I lifted the gun without pointing it at him.

"Remember," I said, "if you start makin' noise, the sock goes back in your mouth. Got it?"

He frowned and nodded. "But I–"

"Shut up. This is gon' be the last time I ask: how did you steal my novel?"

He took a deep breath. "Listen. I don't know what you want from me. Okay? I didn't steal anything from you. I had no idea who you were until you started harassing me on Twitter. Like, I just, I don't know how to get you to believe me. Whatever. Do what you gotta do."

Then he started to cry. He tried to hide it, but I could hear the snot flitting around his nostrils. I wanted to be disgusted or furious, but all I mustered was some reluctant pity. I cut the engine and walked around to his side of the car. I opened the door and grabbed him by the shoulder.

"C'mon," I barked. "Get out." He resisted. "Get the fuck out, I ain't kiddin'." He shifted his center of gravity to the bucket of the seat, so I punched him in the stomach. That loosened him up enough for me to drag him to the pavement by his shirt.

It was the time of night when the air gets deep into your lungs, bringing frostiness from hollers and treetops along with it. The overcast was backlit by a faint glow of moonlight, suggesting that we were being watched by some ethereal being, but in this crumbling parking lot near War, West Virginia, isolated and eerily quiet, we were unmistakably alone and I was closer to Rodrigo than I ever could have imagined.

He was on his side, playing dead, and I knew he wouldn't fess up no matter how much I battered him. He had surrendered and was willing to suffer whatever came his way, wrestling with the fact that his life might suddenly be over. He wasn't handling that part of it very well, but I can't say I blame him. There have been moments when I thought it was over for me and the feeling of dread can't be described. Not even close. All in all, Rodrigo was performing better than I had expected.

I nudged him with my foot. "Get up." He didn't move. "You don't wanna be layin' on the ground like a goddamn dog. Have a bit of dignity and get on your feet."

He looked up and made eye contact. "Go fuck yourself."

"Well that ain't very nice."

"Says the guy who's about to kill me."

I let him consider the irony for a few seconds. "I keep askin' you a simple question, and you keep refusin' to answer."

"Jesus Christ," he said. "Just stop already. You're convinced I stole your novel. You're treating it like a universal truth. But it's not true. I don't know what else to tell you."

"You're a stubborn little bastard, ain't you?"

"That makes us exactly the same, doesn't it?"

"You oughta fix your mouth to quit talkin' nonsense."

"Whatever. I'm not ignoring reality just to tell you what you want to hear."

"Oh, suddenly you're too good to lie?"

"Give it a rest. None of my lying had anything to do with you. I was lying to myself."

"Seems even worse to me."

"The audience didn't give me any other choice." I snorted and gave him a kick. "I should be the one mad at you," he continued. "You're trying to claim my greatest accomplishment for yourself."

"Don't project, sparky. It only makes me angrier."

"Like I said, whatever."

I paused to mull over our conversation. I had grown weary of the same back-and-forth. Rodrigo was useless. He would offer no regret, no apologies. Whatever I was seeking, I wouldn't find it with him. And yet I wanted to give the guy one more chance. "Maybe somebody's fuckin' with both of us," I conceded.

"That, or you're insane. Hard to say which is more likely."

After all the pleading and groveling he'd done, the son of a bitch was looking up at me with an enormous smirk.

I popped him on top of the head with the gun barrel and he collapsed onto the pavement. I leaned down and grabbed the front of his shirt. "I know what I know," I growled. And then I gave him a series of blows to the face. *Whap whap whap whap*. I could hear him moaning and sobbing as I got into the car.

It was still dark when I got home. I tried to stretch the stiffness out of my back and thighs. At my age, it was a lost cause. I flopped onto my bed, fully clothed, and fell asleep immediately, despite knowing full well that my problem hadn't been solved.

# 13

I woke up the next afternoon and went about my normal business for a while before remembering the events of the prior day. A feeling of dread expanded from my stomach into my extremities. I brewed a pot of coffee and waited for the cops to show up.

They never did. After a few days I allowed myself to believe that Terry and I had gotten away with it. It seemed like more than a miracle, maybe something akin to a supernatural occurrence.

Rodrigo's abduction made headlines, but he didn't have a ton to say about it. I figured he'd for sure rat me out and I'd wake up to a SWAT team busting down my front door. But no. His story was that he didn't know the identity of his assailants. I started to feel a bit guilty for attacking him as a liar. Well, I felt a bit guilty about the attack. His lying wasn't a problem this time.

It's not that Rodrigo didn't play up the situation. He did what any other minor celebrity would do: carried on about the traumatic ordeal, humble-bragged about his injuries, made some noises about not looking for carceral solutions to economic and social problems. But he wasn't bombastic or overblown. For the first time, I noticed a certain coyness, maybe even humility, in his demeanor. This Rodrigo was different. He wasn't enjoying the attention nearly as much as he should have been.

So, anyway, the cops never showed up and I started assuming that we were in the clear. That was the strangest thing of all. I didn't know how Rodrigo had gotten hold of my novel, but was equally confused as to why he didn't identify his kidnapper. With our Twitter history, it would have been a slam-dunk case for the prosecution. Not that I would have denied involvement. Driving back from War, I decided that I'd accept whatever consequences came my way. I wouldn't rat out Terry. His life, however worthless it might seem to outsiders, still had value. Not mine, though. I was simply sucking away resources from worthier creatures.

You'd think I was thrilled to not have been caught, but I was mostly apathetic. I couldn't figure out Rodrigo's angle in keeping my secret and after a while I quit thinking about it altogether.

Maybe you're wondering why I didn't kill him. Hell, I'm wondering the same thing. It wasn't because I was scared of getting caught. It wasn't for moral reasons, either. I can't say exactly why I left him in that dark, rundown parking lot in the backwoods of West Virginia. It felt like that's where he needed to be, I guess. And it felt like I needed to get out of there. The logical part of my brain wanted to empty the cartridge into his face, but something stopped me from squeezing the trigger, something inside the unknown parts of my brain that resisted logical solutions. I've spent plenty of time sorting it out since the kidnapping and I reckon I was scared that murder would take away my life, as well.

Soon enough I was back to the usual routine: teaching composition sections, inflating grades for the sake of convenience, and enjoying an occasional evening of drink. I deleted my Twitter and Facebook accounts and put aside my literary aspirations.

And that was that. Rodrigo and I had fought our way into an unspoken peace.

# 14

Terry called and texted a few times, but I ignored him. I guess I was still a bit paranoid, after all. I didn't have anything against Terry and assumed he wasn't mad at me. We'd spent large chunks of our adulthood ignoring each other. Now it seems pretty certain I'll never see him again.

That's just how it is with people like us. Our bonds are really strong and fragile at the same time. Nobody else understands the peculiar culture we grew up in, but it's not a culture any of us is eager to claim. And the only way to escape a culture is to avoid the people who understand it.

None of this shit makes much sense to me, anyway. I wanted to be K'iche', or at least Guatemalan, but it was impossible. Rodrigo managed to do it and I almost shot his ass as a result. It would have been the merciful move. I debased a thousand norms and customs by keeping the bullets in place.

I remember we used to play basketball at a Catholic church on the West Virginia side. It was a compact stone building near downtown with what used to be an old school or something across the parking lot. On the top floor was a basketball court, musty and dark, with cinderblock walls and a stage on one end. It was regulation size, though, with real hardwood. One of our friends went to the church and had arranged for the priest, who lived somewhere in the building, to open the court for us after school. All we had to do was listen to little sermons about abstinence and the Holy Spirit.

I think the priest liked having us around. We were always some combination of the same ten, eleven people. We didn't share our secret with anyone or else half the school would have turned up. Depending on the numbers, we played three-on-three half court or five-on-five full, winning team stays up. The priest, Father Ia-something-or-other—I can't remember the name, but know it started with an I and was very Italian-sounding—ran with us. He was about six-two, still pretty young, and the motherfucker could ball. He'd throw 'bows and talk smack and then gather us around for a lesson on the evil of drugs or the importance of prayer.

Like I said, we'd have put up with pretty much anything to have access to an indoor basketball court, so we nodded along and pretended to take in the wisdom. And then not a mile down the road we'd open beer cans and pray to get our hands on some easy drugs. The priest had to have known.

The funny thing is, one of those sermons actually impressed me and I remember it to this day. The priest was banging on about the importance of faith when Slop Bucket butted in to ask, "Um, 'scuse me, sir, why do we gotta be wastin' time on some'n that can't be proven?" We all leaned away from Slop Bucket in shock. It was nothing for us to hotbox cigarettes behind the heavy curtains on the stage or sneak into the building, looking for something to steal, but Slop Bucket's question felt like a step too far.

Father Whatever didn't seem to mind, though. He smiled and said, "That's an excellent question. I'm glad you asked it." We grumbled in surprise.

"I'll explain it to you boys this way," he continued. "Faith is inherently mysterious. We don't believe a testable hypothesis–a rock you pick up and feel with your fingers, a science experiment you can run in a lab. We believe in the abstract. That's why faith is so special. It requires us to be vulnerable and devoted. Do you understand what I mean?"

We nodded even though I was pretty sure that only two or three of us, tops, knew what he meant.

"That don't make no sense," Slop Bucket said. Again, we leaned away from him, as if he were more radioactive than his nickname. Slop Bucket had never shown this type of enthusiasm in school. Just goes to show that people will surprise you if you give them the chance.

"Why not?" the priest said, without hostility.

"'Cause how can a man be devoted to a story he don't believe?"

"That's the beautiful thing about it. The joy is in the unknowing."

"Nah, I wanna know whether some'n's real or not."

"You wouldn't be able to question something if it weren't real."

"I get what you're sayin', uh, Father? Father, right? But that ain't what I meant."

"You're confusing reality and truth. I understand what you're getting at. I suggest that you read scripture and pray. Think hard about what you're reading. In time you'll see that faith can't exist without mystery. And it's the mystery that makes faith so rewarding."

When we left, I made sure to ride in the same car with Slop Bucket. I wanted to continue the discussion. I slid into the backseat next to him and a few minutes into the drive slapped his arm and said, "What the hell was you gettin' all worked up about with that priest?"

Both of us waited for the boys up front to say something, but they weren't paying attention. Finally, Slop Bucket said, "That guy's full of shit."

"So? That wasn't no reason to argue with him. What if he don't let us use the court no more?"

"I ain't worried 'bout that."

"You should be, dumbass."

"Nah, he liked my questions. Didn't you see the way he was grinnin'?"

"What was up with them questions, anyway? You started gettin' all philosophical and whatnot."

"The way I see it, you gotta give a man a good reason if you want'm to believe in some'n."

I think I mentioned already that, despite his unfortunate nickname, Slop Bucket was pretty darn precocious, even though everyone treated him like a run-of-the-mill idiot.

"So what you're sayin' is belief don't need to be a mystery?"

Suddenly we heard a bang and were thrust forward with enormous force. The driver had been fishing for a cigarette and crashed straight into a telephone pole. Slop Bucket was bleeding from his nose and mouth. My face had bounced off the headrest in front of me and then ricocheted into the window. The side of my head felt like it had just been slapped with an open hand. All four of us were groaning and panting and cussing under our breath.

I took it as a sign that, God or no God, I'd just have to be content with mystery.

# 15

It was a blustery morning midway through the spring semester and I lumbered across campus to teach my first class. Instructors always got the 8 a.m. sections; not even seniority among my peers could get me out of them. The red brick dominating Radford's campus couldn't cheer up the cold, cloudy atmosphere. Some flurries flitted back and forth in the swirling wind.

As expected, the classroom was half-empty. I took attendance each morning, but the students had already figured out it was perfunctory. This morning they looked like cadavers that were extra dead. Most of them were severely underdressed. That's how college kids are, I guess. They either don't feel the cold like old people do, or they're willing to suffer to fit in. It's pretty good training, at least. Suffering for the sake of social cohesion will be their main takeaway from college no matter how little or hard they study.

I took my time sorting out papers on the lectern, letting the friction warm my fingers. As usual, a few students chatted with me before the lesson: TV shows, weather, March Madness, the usual shit.

"Hey professor," one of the students said as I was about to begin. "We're reading a book called *Coyote Road* in one of my other classes. You ever hear of it?"

I tensed up. "Is it any good?"

"Yeah. Like, I hate reading–sorry, Mr. T, but it's true–and it was pretty cool. I actually finished it."

I hate being called Mr. T. Some students think it's cute. But this time I was annoyed by other things. I composed myself and said, "I read it while it was still in draft."

"For real?"

"Believe it or not."

The student kept talking excitedly but I couldn't understand him. He sounded like Charlie Brown's teacher. Static prickled throughout my toes and fingertips and pain began shooting down my left arm. I gripped the lectern as dizziness set in. I was having trouble drawing air into my lungs. A moment later I was on the ground, conscious but incapacitated. I could sense a bunch of people standing above me, asking if I was okay. I couldn't speak. Soon the room went dark.

I woke up to paramedics hoisting me onto a stretcher. The students were gathered around, their heads craned to get a good view of my demise. Suddenly I felt fine and said so to the nearest paramedic. He told me to settle down and relax, that we'd be at the hospital in no time.

"No, seriously, I'm fine," I insisted. Then I raised my voice to address the students. "I'm fine, y'all. Everthing's good."

"Shhh, go ahead and lay back down."

"Really, there's no need to go to the hospital."

The paramedics hoisted up the stretcher and began walking. I didn't like being strapped down.

"Quick trip to the hospital and we'll get you back home in no time," one of the paramedics said.

"I don't know what in the world happened."

"Prolly just a panic attack, but we gotta get you tested, make sure everything's okay."

I quit arguing and let my head rest on the stretcher. As the paramedics moved me through the hallway, I stared at the long fluorescent lights attached to the ceiling. They alternated with cream plaster to give the impression of a psych ward or prison. As we got into the elevator, the tingling returned to my extremities and all I wanted to do was sleep until the world made sense again.

It was right then, amid the vibrating hum of a descending elevator carrying me to a vehicle of the infirm, that I resolved to never again entertain the existence of one Rodrigo Fucking Suarez.

# 16

Now, you're probably thinking, "Goddammit, Jerry, you can't end the story like that. We need to know what the hell happened." No need to worry. I don't intend to leave you hanging.

Problem is, there's really not much to tell. I'll give it a go, anyhow, because I hate the idea of disappointing you.

I finished out the semester at Radford and then headed south. I sold my house and car and anything else that would put cash in my pocket. Once in Guatemala, I set up in a small apartment in the capital. Most of the people I had known when I first lived in Central America were gone and I wasn't interested in finding those who remained.

After settling in, I ventured out to the countryside and visited the K'iche' village where I had spent so much time. The people who hadn't migrated remembered me and it wasn't long before I began staying the night. Not much had changed since the old days: the houses stayed modest and farm animals still roamed the street. There were fewer people. That was the most notable difference. Nobody seemed to mind my return. I caught up with the old folks and went about trying to make myself useful. I couldn't replace the loved ones who had left, but I was a living body and that was enough to override the villagers' natural suspicion. I knew that trust was a rare commodity and worked hard to earn it from the locals. I did whatever was needed. Only in that verdant, isolated village did I ever feel a sense of civic responsibility.

You can't stay in that sort of place otherwise. Visions of a shared destiny are the difference between survival or disappearance. I was most comfortable around Doña Justina not because she was familiar to me, but because of her unfamiliarity. I wasn't looking for a surrogate mother or a new friend. She wasn't offering those roles, anyway. Nor was she offering the unknown. Hell, she wasn't offering anything but her presence and that alone finally got me the elite education I'd always missed out on, one that required no lectures or evaluations. Doña Justina might have spent ten hours a day wondering about the meaning of her life, but she already knew the truth of my reality. It was a story told to her long ago.

She had grown skinnier and a few threads of silver weaved through her hair, but otherwise she was just the same. I brought her groceries and little knickknacks and gave her the money I earned to distribute as she saw fit. If people complained about her methods, I never heard anything about it. I tried to stay out of internal drama, just as I never attended, or was invited to attend, various council and community meetings.

Nobody interrogated me about why I was there, though Doña Justina's curiosity eventually got the better of her.

"Why you come, Mister?" she asked about a week after I showed back up.

"I'm ashamed."

"Yes." She nodded without any change in her expression. "Yes."

She continued to arrange the movement of people in and out of the village. The idea was that when people left, money would return. That was the exchange. I suppose everyone would have preferred for the people to stay, but without money there wouldn't be anyone at all. The arrangement was completely averse to Doña Justina and yet she had it down pat. Human beings disappeared into a lush, treacherous horizon in order for their history to remain. It was necessary, for sure, but it still seemed like a shitty bargain.

Doña Justina clearly had no problem with emigration, but seemingly had no desire to get out of there herself. I wanted to hear more, so I asked one day. "Why have you never gone north?"

"Maybe I have."

That's all I could get out of her. I figured that Doña Justina had moved around the world plenty even if she'd never actually left Guatemala. I don't know how to explain it. Basically, I started noticing the difference between where you are and where you exist. It's not something I'd ever considered before, but when the idea first came into my head the entire world changed shape. If Doña Justina left, then a lot of history might go with her. And when history goes away, the future feels a whole lot more uncertain. You don't need computers and cars and all that crap to have certainty. You just need to know a thing or two that's unknown to everyone else.

Whether by force or choice, the K'iche' knew a thing or two, which explained why I could be seen as suspicious but not threatening. Don't get me wrong, the lack of trust was warranted and not just because I was an outsider.

Things were tense when I arrived. It was hard for anyone to look at a white face and not associate it with multinational corporations. And people of every color were potential informants. Still, I found the environment less stressful than a college campus.

Indigenous activists and other campesinos were still murdered regularly and relations with the central government were at best nonexistent. A lot of villages organized against the expansion of zinc and nickel mines, which brought repression and reprisal from the army. The lakes were turning red with industrial runoff and fish were dying in enormous numbers. My village was far from most of the action, but everyone kept aware of the goings-on in other areas and the place was engulfed by an aura of foreboding. Destroying a village or two was an easy way for politicians to increase their popularity among domestic bigwigs and foreign sponsors.

I knew that beautiful landscapes could be a source of misery for their inhabitants. Hills often have minerals and bringing those minerals to the surface requires a lot of cheap labor. But the Guatemalan countryside suffered an entirely different level of insecurity. It's like the Indians and peasants expected the worst, probably because they'd seen it already.

I devoted myself to the trade in crafts and turned over all profits to Doña Justina. My savings would get me by for a while and I figured I'd eventually find some way to make money that didn't feel dirty. I knew I'd always have a meal and a place to sleep and that made it easier to transport inventory between village and city. I was a living microloan for the village, without the debt burden.

After I had reacclimated to the pace and structure of life in Guatemala, I joined some protests, which were really intense—none of that touchy-feely stuff ending with dinner reservations. These events were stark and serious; you could feel all kinds of violent energy surrounding them. It was the first time in my life that I had done anything resembling activism. It was the first time I cared about an issue that had nothing to do with self-gratification. Basically, it was the first time I thought of myself as a decent human being. I liked the action and was used to dicey situations, so I wasn't afraid. I just had to keep my own behavior in check. No punching, no trash-talking. Doing so would get innocent people killed. Keep my head straight, try to be dignified. The demonstrators always put me in the front. They supposed that the police were less likely to shoot a gringo.

They were right, but only to an extent. After a while, soldiers got itchy and even the dumbest among them could figure out that I wasn't anyone important. They tried to avoid me when busting heads, but they didn't let me slow them down. If I caught an ass-beating along with the riffraff, then so be it.

Those experiences changed me. I wasn't marching with the K'iche' to be seen as a hero or to have good stories to tell at BT's; I did it because it felt like the right thing to do. Earning your keep was a big thing back in Appalachia. I decided this was the best way to do it.

Anyway, I'm never seeing BT's again. I'm never seeing any part of the United States again, not if I can help it. I'm not worried about getting nabbed for my adventure with Rodrigo. More like I want out of the place that allowed people like me and Rodrigo to exist. For my entire life up to this point, I thought desecration was the height of culture. Down here, in a different set of mountains, I can be a scumbag without also being a terrible person.

The main reason I'd returned was to start another novel. I'd intended to handwrite this one, but it never quite got off the ground and I lost interest. I began learning K'iche' and joining various ceremonies. I took long walks in the jungle, always damp, always dense. My lungs acclimated to the elevation. I began to make sense of the land.

And that's where you find me now, in an isolated K'iche' village filled with sustenance and low on possessions.

I don't know what the fuck I'm doing, exactly. I'm here and life is generally pleasant, but it's not like I have a specific purpose. I'm just existing, I guess, trying to unlearn a lifetime of noxious habits.

I think I'm making progress—not progress as I always understood the word, but a kind of retrogression into something more uncultured and compassionate, if that makes any sense. A few weeks ago, I was in the city making a delivery to a few shops and looking for specialty items to bring to the village. I had just withdrawn some cash, the equivalent of $100, and was walking along a dusty street at the edge of downtown. The decaying brown architecture of the city put me in a good mood, despite the new skyline of luxury apartment buildings, and by that point I could navigate its jagged spaces as deftly as a local.

A beggar sat cross-legged on the edge of the street, surrounded by food wrappers and cigarette butts and damp splotches that smelled of piss and motor oil. He held out a paper cup that appeared to be empty. The few pedestrians passing by ignored him. Coarse purple scars covered his cheeks and his eyes were thin in the classic Mayan style. I stopped to give him a handful of change. As I peeked into the cup, the beggar grabbed my shirt and pulled me toward him. Before I could react, he pressed the tip of a knife against my neck, just below the Adam's apple. I felt the metal pierce the outer layer of skin.

"All your fucking money," he said.

His mouth was only inches from my face. I wanted to look around and see if anyone was nearby, but knew that nobody would intervene. The guy's fierce black eyes looked almost childlike. His expression was more innocent than mean. Still, I didn't doubt that he would run the blade through my esophagus if I gave him any reason.

I could have grabbed his arm below the bicep and squeezed before he had a chance to stab me. I was standing above him and without the knife to my neck he would have made an easy target. Instead I kept my eyes fixated on his and pulled the cash out of my pocket. I handed it to him and raised my brows as if to say, "Okay, you can let me go now." He stuffed the bills into his jacket and then scampered into a nearby alley.

I stood there, shaken and confused. It wasn't the assault itself that had me upset. It was that I had no objection to giving the guy my money. It's not something that's supposed to happen; giving up money is a bitch move. But there I was, with an opportunity to maim the thief, and I didn't want to do it. My impulse was to let him go and hope that he'd put the cash to good use. That alone would catch me a whooping back home.

So, yeah, I guess you could call it progress, but it's not what most people mean when they use the word. Their version of progress requires the kind of bloodshed I wanted to avoid.

Whatever you want to call it, I was too far gone to consider a return. I had nothing left in Virginia, anyway. Mama had died a long time ago and Terry and Slop Bucket and the other guys weren't friends so much as fixtures in an unchanging landscape. The only relationship of substance I had left behind was with Missy and she stopped talking to me well before I left the country. I never told her where I was going. Hell, I didn't tell her I was going anywhere at all.

Hard to say that our bond was anything more than superficial. We were old college acquaintances and professional colleagues, sort of. Missy occupied a higher echelon. We pretended there wasn't any difference, though. Looking back on it, I realized that I wasn't very nice to her. I was smart-alecky and cynical and didn't say anything to suggest that I respected her. Such behavior didn't do much harm to our relationship because it's what she expected of men from our part of the world even though we came off much better in her presentations of the region. I suppose her admiration for Rodrigo finally wised her up to my rottenness. We weren't connected by love or compassion or anything that makes a relationship durable and still she was the only family I had.

Here's the funny thing about Missy: she wasn't the type to forget, so it was only a matter of time before she tried to find me. Eventually she located me in the village's small internet café, a garage-sized box with three consoles, usually occupied by teenagers playing video games. She didn't know it, though. But I noticed that she requested a receipt showing I had opened her email.

> Dear Jerry:
>
> I don't know where this message will find you, or even if you're alive. I pray to God that you are. I hope you'll see fit to let me know.
>
> You'll have to excuse me if I ramble. I have a lot to say to you but I don't really know what to say. I don't even know if I'm talking to anyone.
>
> Things are fine in Radford. The English Department is hiring for two positions, one in composition and one in digital humanities. It's pretty exciting for us. I had to work hard on the dean to make it happen. I always wished that you'd just get your PhD because I'm certain we would have found a line for you. But anyway.
>
> Also, I've finally convinced the provost to make Appalachian Studies a full-fledged major. It's my dream come true! I'll be too

busy to do anything else for the next few years, but it's worth it. There's so much potential and I just love our students to death. If you ever show up again, I insist that you come to my class and give a guest lecture.

In more personal news, my mother passed away a few months ago. I'm still recovering. But she lived a good long life. She died in her sleep, so she didn't suffer. Remember when you visited Tazewell with me that one weekend? She always laughed about how you ate like nine scones in one sitting. She was so tickled that you liked them so much. I never had the heart to tell her that you were stoned out of your mind. I thought you might like to know that she remembered you all the way to the end.

There's something I've been wanting to tell you, although I don't really know how. So I'll just say it: I looked into Rodrigo Suarez and it seems that you weren't totally wrong about him. That doesn't excuse the way you behaved toward me, but I understand now that you weren't completely crazy and I apologize for not believing you. I still don't know what happened and probably never will. Whatever, though. I do think it's funny how he disappeared from public life after that crazy incident in Bluefield. Did he fake his kidnapping? So weird.

Well, Jerry, I guess I've talked enough. I do hope that you're in good shape to read it. I'm a bit worried about you. Despite everything, you're really missed around here. It still feels weird that you're gone. This place just isn't the same without you.

Love,
Missy

I logged off and headed outside. It was near dusk, a beautiful hour in the tropics, and the late-afternoon breeze was coming in from the mountains. Debris and dead foliage tumbled across the village square. I passed the usual assortment of old men sitting outside ramshackle buildings, having conversations without actually talking.

A large nimbus cloud, bright white with cotton-like puffs, covered half the sky. Beside it, a pastiche of pink and purple spread across the horizon.

I thought about Missy as I headed to my encampment, but quickly lost interest as I imagined her among Radford's semi-Georgian architecture, flanked by a dark and light side and filled with gaudy flower beds, with students glued to their smartphones, with administrators cruising proudly in their electric cars.

Even though I'm running out of money and have no prospects for anything that could be called a career, I can't say I miss Appalachia. Down here, I don't have the burden of any fakery; I only have an obligation to not be myself.

And that's how the story ends, with me sitting outside a home built of canvas and chaparro branches, staring at a sunset increasingly obscured by a mass of billowing clouds. I reckon you could say that the story begins here, but we don't need to dick around with semantics.

They say that a thief likes to revisit the scene of the crime. It sounds about right to me. But maybe the thief doesn't always go back to steal; maybe some thieves simply want to restore the original desire. I don't really know. I've surrendered to mystery. See, back home I knew pretty much everything a person needed to know. It was a dangerous state of being, because knowing everything means that you understand nothing at all.

What else can I say? Despite being stuck in a million pastoral fantasies, Missy was right about one thing: it's probably best for everyone that I'm gone, wherever it is I'm said to exist, but absence sure does a damn sad number on a person's sense of place in this world.

## ACKNOWLEDGMENTS

Tremendous gratitude to Malav Kanuga and the team at Common Notions Press, who constantly reaffirm my decision to stay away from corporate publishing.

Tremendous gratitude as well to Diana, whose enthusiasm for this novel provided even more joy than writing it. Thanks for always embracing the Appalachian in me and the greater whole in which it is situated.

Badr Makhoul and Ermela Morena, each uncommonly perceptive, read drafts of the novel with great care and compassion. I remain in their debt.

Although I can't replicate his brilliance, this novel was influenced by the work of Jim Thompson, the underappreciated, oft-ignored madman of American modernism.

There is a politics in this novel, of course, which I will leave for readers to discern according to their proclivities, but I should like to be candid enough to dedicate *Jerry and Rodrigo Go to War* to Indigenous nations everywhere.

## ABOUT THE AUTHOR

**Steven Salaita** is a scholar and writer based in Egypt. He is the author of nine nonfiction books, most notably *Inter/Nationalism: Decolonizing Native America and Palestine*, *Israel's Dead Soul*, and the recently published memoir, *An Honest Living*. He currently teaches at the American University in Cairo. His previous novel is *Daughter, Son, Assassin*. His essays can be found at stevesalaita.com.

# ABOUT COMMON NOTIONS

Common Notions is a publishing house and programming platform that fosters new formulations of living autonomy. We aim to circulate timely reflections, clear critiques, and inspiring strategies that amplify movements for social justice.

Our publications trace a constellation of critical and visionary meditations on the organization of freedom. By any media necessary, we seek to nourish the imagination and generalize common notions about the creation of other worlds beyond state and capital. Inspired by various traditions of autonomism and liberation—in the US and internationally, historical and emerging from contemporary movements—our publications provide resources for a collective reading of struggles past, present, and to come.

Common Notions regularly collaborates with political collectives, militant authors, radical presses, and maverick designers around the world. Our political and aesthetic pursuits are dreamed and realized with Antumbra Designs.

www.commonnotions.org
info@commonnotions.org